Counting Midnight

By

J.J. Massa

Published by
Melange Books, LLC
White Bear Lake, MN 55110
www.melange-books.com

ISBN 978-1-61235-096-7

Credits

Editor: Nancy Schumacher
Copy Editor: Mae Powers
Format Editor: Taylor Evans
Cover Artist: A. Bratt

Counting Midnight
By
J.J. Massa

Vasile Velicescu is finally finding peace after the death of his long time lover. But when he interviews a young woman who looks exactly like his lost love, he is angry, yet elated to have found her once again.

Nina Caruthers knew she shouldn't have taken the job at Velicescu Finance. At first her smooth and sexy boss makes her feel things, familiar things that she can't understand. What is this hold he has on her?

Dedication:
To my family—you're always there for me.

www.jjmassa.com

Also by J.J. Massa in the Mélange Digest on sale at:
www.melange-books.com:

Nailed: Terry Lee Derby is a builder, a simple man with simple plans, until one small, hard working woman, Sida Zhou, nailed him down, permanently.

Also by J.J. Massa:
The Montgomery Family Werewolves:
A howlingly good series.

Counting Midnight
By
J.J. Massa

Chapter One

Once again, Vasile Velicescu made his way into his office at his usual time of four-thirty in the afternoon. His mood was as black as it was every other day – as it had been for the last two years. For this reason, he was surprised that his generally sensible secretary dared to approach him.

"I thought you knew better than to bother me when I am having a bad mood, Beverly!" he barked. "Do you, too, need replacing?" he growled. His administrative assistant had been the last to go.

"Sir," she said hesitantly. "Sir," she said just a little more strongly, "There's a young lady that Human Relations and the Client Team want you to hire. Sir, they like her very much." She took a deep breath. "Mr. Velicescu, please just talk to her. They say our company needs her, sir. They think she could be your new assistant."

Vasile looked at his secretary and then glanced to the seating area she had indicated. He literally stumbled backward. He felt like the breath had been knocked from him. There she was.

Two years of agony and loneliness had passed for him and finally he was beginning to accept the disappearance of Nina Caruthers, his longtime lover, from his life. But there she was. It was Nina—it had to be. He had no doubt. How could that be possible? He'd been positive she was dead.

Stunned, he took her resume and the folder assembled by his staff and turned toward his office, overcome with memories.

Vasile remembered interrupting her brutal rape at the hands of two violent young men. Nina had been only sixteen years old, then. He'd killed her attackers after first feeding on them. That was eleven years ago.

Gently, he'd wrapped her in a cloak and stayed with her until the police had arrived. Some impulse had caused him to discreetly check on her at the hospital later that night. After that he'd come at night when no visitors were allowed, entering her room and holding her in his arms. He'd felt drawn to her and his presence had seemed to soothe her.

Vasile jerked his mind back to the present long enough to address his secretary again.

"Beverly, send her in after five minutes and get us some coffee," he growled.

He turned from Beverly's desk and walked into his own office. Lowering himself into his executive chair, he began scanning through her resume. Yes, it was her—it was his Nina.

He'd never realized that Nina had achieved a Bachelor's degree in Economics, another Bachelor's in Cyrillic Languages with a minor in Romance Languages and a Master's degree in business law. As an administrative assistant, she was more than he could have ever hoped for and completely, through no fault of his, she had turned up on his doorstep.

Looking back Vasile reflected that he had never said one word to Nina. Often, during the first year after the rape, he'd held her and sat with her at night. But when she left for college, he'd thought to let her go. Until then, he'd fed from her but never had he coupled with her.

Absently, he'd decided to keep her for his lover. He

went looking for her near her college and found her walking along the beach one night, alone. That was the first time he'd kissed her. His body had hardened instantly with an urgent hunger. Fighting the urge to make love to her there in the sand, he'd gently put her away from him.

Shortly after that, he'd sent her dorm mate away and tenderly soothed Nina into making love. She'd been so afraid. He'd loved her carefully and tenderly for hours.

Vasile knew that, as a vampire, he had all of eternity to meet people, learn about them, love them – if that were possible, and lose them. He'd never embedded himself into Nina's mind.

She had a strong mind and a natural block. He had decided that she was to be his lover. He would protect her from danger but he would not be part of her day-to-day life nor would she be part of his. For those reasons, Vasile had never scanned Nina's mind. He never took the time to learn more about her. When she left him, he couldn't find her and had no idea where to look.

He kept an ear on Beverly's conversation with Nina. As he listened to the two women speaking, Beverly cautioned the girl that she'd be going in while the boss was in a bad mood.

Vasile heard Nina ask Beverly, "Do you know what Vasile means in English?" Beverly said she didn't know. "It means Basil." He heard Beverly chuckle delightedly. "I'm pretty sure Basil won't bite me. I'm not afraid of him." His secretary worried over the girl a few more minutes.

"He doesn't act much like a Basil, though." Beverly cautioned her. "Doesn't look like one, either."

Vasile heard Nina tell his secretary, "Don't worry, please. The worst has already happened to me. I'm going to be okay."

For the first time in centuries, Vasile felt like crying. The feeling was at war with the towering anger he'd felt when he first saw her sitting there. Even so, rage still bubbled inside of him. He wasn't done with Nina Caruthers.

His Nina had a soft, sweet, husky voice and a mischievous sense of humor. But, she'd left him. He had thought her dead. Now, here she was in his offices, applying for employment.

She wouldn't get away from him again. He didn't know if he would punish her or how, but she would not get away.

He didn't look up when she entered the room. He was still gripped with rage at her for leaving him. The fact that she let him think she was dead infuriated him further. Vasile sat reading her paperwork, forcing himself to show no emotion. With difficulty, he kept his anger in check.

She gracefully lowered herself into a chair near his desk and sat quietly. He watched her covertly but didn't say anything. His mind reached out to hers, finding definite changes. He could feel her natural shield but it was not nearly as strong as it had been.

Beverly brought the coffee in a minute later. Nina thanked her for it and indicted that she could leave. Vasile would have been annoyed by such impertinence usually, but this time, he said nothing.

Finally, he could ignore her no longer. He could feel her scrutiny. Looking up, he found her eyes traveling over his face. He smiled in amusement when she met his eyes. His little Nina was "checking him out". He probed her mind wondering what she thought of him. It seemed that the young lady liked what she saw. She was embarrassed to be caught looking. A little of his fury melted away–only a little.

"Welcome to Velicescu Finance, Miss Caruthers. I understand you are interested in employment with us," he told her, focusing on her face. He'd need to look in her eyes to embed his "link" into her thoughts.

She sat still and quiet for a few more seconds. He

didn't quite know what she was thinking yet—she seemed to be organizing her thoughts. She was pale and more than that, she looked fragile. He noticed that her hair was a good deal shorter than it had been two years ago. Had it been cut?

"Thank you, Mr. Velicescu. Other members of your administrative staff have asked me to come aboard. It is your endorsement we await. Of course, we all understand that your vision for the future may be different than that of your staff."

She waited patiently having given him the perfect escape. Now it was up to him. He stared at her over his tented fingers. He could tell that she didn't know who he was.

Searching for answers in her mind, he found many changes in her. Her mind seemed raw, bruised.

Nina's forehead furrowed. "Mr. Velicescu, have we met before?" He arched a brow at her. A blush stole up her cheeks. "I'm sorry, sir. I'm sure we haven't." He could feel a small ache bloom behind her eyes.

"Miss Caruthers? It says here that you left your last job rather abruptly. Although you have done some consulting during the last six months, there is quite a gap in your history." Looking over the papers, he said, "Just over a year and a half. Can you explain that?" Vasile fixed his icy black gaze on her blue-green eyes.

"I took an impromptu trip abroad. I was to be gone only two weeks. While I was there, I was involved in a catastrophic accident. My recovery has taken a very long time." He could tell she had practiced saying that.

"Were others involved in this accident, Nina?" he probed softly, reaching for her mind, compelling her to answer. She attempted to block him, but she was still remarkably weak. She didn't seem to even know that he was searching her mind or that she was resisting. He found that quite curious.

"Yes, many people were involved. My g-g-grandmother perished." Her eyes filled with tears. She cleared her throat and shook her head.

As he explored her thoughts, he heard the screeching of metal wheels and saw an image of an old woman crushed beneath a train car. He heard Nina's screams for her.

"Why did you take this trip, Nina?" he purred. He would have his answers now. These last two years without knowing was enough.

A tear dripped down her cheek. She touched it, surprised. "Nina, tell me," he commanded her silkily. He gave her no choice. She had to respond.

"I had to think about some things. I needed to get away for a little while and clear my mind," she said just above a whisper.

"What things did you need to think about? Why did you need to get away?" his soothing voice coerced her answers.

"My friend, Jason, told me he loved me. I was lonely and the man I loved didn't love me." She drew in a deep, trembling breath.

Something loosened in his chest. "Had you planned to return?" he asked her, his black eyes focused on hers.

"Yes, sir. I was coming back," she whispered.

Once again, he foraged for information. "Tell me of your injuries, little Nina." his smooth, accented, hypnotizing voice tugged at her.

Against her will, Nina complied. "I was in a coma for many months," she whispered, her voice cracking.

So that's why she'd seemed dead. Her mind had shut down to heal itself. More of the rage he'd been feeling for so long dissolved.

"I had a head injury; my jaw was broken, some of my ribs were broken, my clavicle was broken and my spleen ruptured and was removed. I was pinned in a farmer's muddy field and suffered a systemic infection that I must

9

still care for." She struggled to maintain her composure. It was obvious she did not like talking about the accident or the state of her health.

"And your health now?" His eyes bored into hers.

"Mostly, I'm fine, Mr. Velicescu. I am careful of infections and sometimes migraines plague me, but nothing too serious." He could feel her struggle to hold back.

"Nina," his black velvet voice warned her. "You are not to lie to me. Your health now, Nina?" he growled.

"The infection always threatens me," her voice shook. "I have to be careful. If I get sick again, it could be life threatening." She so clearly didn't want to tell him these things. "But absenteeism won't be a problem, sir. My later hours seem to agree with yours," she said immediately, attempting to placate him.

He probed her mind. What was she trying to hide? Nothing she revealed so far had given him more than a clue. But he knew there was something more. He suspected that her health was much more precarious than she was telling him.

"Nina? What are you hiding from me, hmmm?" his seductive, black satin voice flowed over her, coercing her, forcing her to answer.

"I, I, I'm not..." she whispered.

"Sweet little Nina, what is the secret you dread so? You are powerless to hide your fears from me, you will tell me." His beguiling voice wrapped around her like cashmere and silk.

"I must keep the infection at bay. It is similar to Malaria. It is very unstable." Her voice was a strangled whisper. "I shouldn't have come here. I should have stayed away and let it happen." She stood and made to turn for the door.

"But you did come, my Nina." His words poured over her, warm and gentle, "You are with me again, and I will let nothing, not even death, take you from me this time."

He smiled and stood. "Miss Caruthers, thank you for joining our organization." He walked around the desk with his hand extended. "Is there a Mr. Caruthers we should welcome?" He carefully concealed the instant fury he felt at the idea of another man touching her.

Nina turned toward him. She seemed surprised to be facing the wrong direction. Vasile took her hand in his. He felt her break out in goose bumps.

"No, sir," she forced out, "there is no Mr. Caruthers."

"Nina, has any other man touched you intimately?" He cupped her chin in his hand and trained his disturbing gaze on her.

"Sir?" her brow knit as his thumb caressed her cheek.

"Have you let another man touch what is mine, little Nina?" his dark, velvet smooth voice stroked her.

"I've only ever wanted one man intimately. I have been celibate since the accident. He, he didn't…I, I couldn't …" she was becoming agitated now.

"Be calm," he murmured, his thumb moving to caress her lower lip.

He searched her mind. She missed him. She thought he must not want her anymore. Vasile found a vague memory of growling in her mind–she thought of it as his anger. In her thoughts, she worried that he believed she'd deserted him. The last of his ire seeped away.

He pulled her to him and kissed her forehead. With the wave of a hand, he locked his office door. Gently, he tipped her head up and pressed it to his shoulder. Resting his lips against her racing pulse, Vasile touched it with his tongue.

"Shh, be at peace, my Nina. I am with you again."

His hot tongue traced the rapid pulse along the column of her throat. Up. Down. He sunk his fangs deep and drank from her.

His body was hard in an instant. Fighting the urge to

feast on her life force, Vasile took only enough to have her inside of him. He would not lose her another time. His tongue closed the tiny wounds.

Stepping away from her, he held her hand as if he'd only just begun to shake it, and pumped it again. Dropping her hand, Vasile guided her toward the door. He flicked a finger at it and it unlocked before he reached it.

"You will not go away from me again, Nina," he purred in his mesmerizing voice.

"No, of course not, Mr. Velicescu," she said in confusion.

He watched her as she left. So, she had not been leaving him. That was good–good for her, anyway. Still, she couldn't be allowed to come and go as she pleased. True, he was embedded in her now. He'd made a path into her mind and he'd sealed it with her blood. He'd instructed her not to leave him and she would be unable to go more than a few miles without telling him.

Would that be enough? What punishment should he mete out to her for leaving him to believe she was dead for two long years? Even now, she would lie to him about her health. Could he trust her?

Looking inward, he saw her step out into the rain and he did his best to shield her from it. Mentally, he tracked her to her home and watched through her eyes as she changed into comfortable clothes.

When she lay down to sleep that evening, he sent her tired body an extra nudge. She needed healing sleep to replace the blood he'd taken and to help her body recover. She was still so weak.

She didn't know he was her mysterious lover. That didn't matter to him though. He had her back and he would not let her go a second time. He wasn't sure why he felt so possessive, but he did. She belonged to him and he would make sure she was his in every way.

* * * *

While she stood in the rain waiting for a cab, Nina reviewed her meeting with her new employer. He was a very disconcerting man.

She had studied Vasile Velicescu from under her lashes. He was sinfully handsome and frighteningly powerful. He had an air of authority about him, but there was more. He seemed to exude danger and mystery.

Taking inventory of his features, she had appreciated what she could see of his hard muscled body and the coal colored hair held back by a leather cord. As she surveyed his face, she'd admired his sensual mouth, strong chin and high cheekbones. His chiseled face was cruel or it was beautiful, she couldn't decide which.

She had felt herself blushing when her gaze moved to his hooded obsidian eyes and found them focused on her. With effort, she'd managed not to squirm in her seat. His eyes were like black magic pools. It had been so hard not to keep staring into them.

Parts of the interview were a little fuzzy to her but she must have done okay because he had approved her employment. When they shook hands, she had felt a shock run through her followed by goose bumps. Just touching this virile and handsome man had brought her to instant arousal.

She was a little surprised and offended that he seemed to think she was planning to leave already. She'd show him that she was a good employee and he'd made the right decision.

Her hours were to be from one in the afternoon to one in the morning most days. That worked well for her because she found herself disoriented for a while when she woke up. She'd learned that many people who'd had a Splenectomy suffered the same side effects. Since she'd be working with banks and companies in other countries, the odd hours were necessary.

Still, her new boss reminded her of her Midnight Guardian. Should she be nervous about that? Her lover had protected her and never hurt her. She missed him so much. He'd always found her in the past. He must not want her anymore. For the millionth time, she wondered if he thought she'd deserted him and if he was angry with her.

She hadn't deserted him. She'd been coming back. During her ill-fated trip, she'd realized that she loved the silent man who came when he wanted and used her body. He'd been the only real lover she'd ever had and the only one she'd ever wanted.

She had made the decision that she would speak to him the next time he came even if it made him angry. It sounded silly but the truth was, she had never heard her lover's voice and had never seen his face. He had only ever come to her in the dark of night with the lights off. She had sometimes wondered if he looked like The Beast or The Phantom of the Opera.

Nina knew she'd need to be careful around her new boss. Aside from the way he made her think of her lover, he posed real dangers to her. He seemed to look right inside her, reading all of her secrets.

Would he fire her if he knew she wouldn't be with him for more than a few years? Could he? *What will he do if he ever finds out how unstable this infection I have really is? Should I have stayed in Moldavia and waited for the end to come?*

Vasile Velicescu had been *very* mad at her for some reason. By the time she'd finished her interview, he seemed calmer but she knew he had been angry. She'd found him very intimidating. *I don't know what I did to make him mad but I never want to do it again.*

After she changed out of her interview clothes, Nina found her old diary. Ever since her rape, she'd kept track of the times she'd seen her Midnight lover. Every single minute of the Midnights they shared was accounted for. She'd kept track of the time he spent with her and even made little notations.

Someday, she'd remember what those notations meant. She'd written 'neck', 'thrt', 'br', and 'lg'. Today, however, she held the old diary for comfort. It was as close as she could get to the only man with whom she had chosen to share her body.

She fell asleep clutching her diary to her chest. She didn't know why she was so tired. Chiding herself for laziness, she slept most of the weekend away.

When Nina crawled out of bed late Monday morning, she felt like she was catching a cold. Her head was pounding but she tried to ignore it. She took some antibiotics and had a cup of hot tea. She didn't want to be under the weather on her first day of work.

Chapter Two

On Monday afternoon, Vasile arrived at work knowing that Nina would be attending the administrative staff meeting. While the urge to go to her during the weekend had been nearly overpowering, he'd somehow overcome it. It angered him that he had so little discipline when it came to this woman. She'd been his for nearly a decade before her disappearance. He hadn't felt this strongly then. *Of course, perhaps that is the reason I lost her. I ignored my need for her and let her live unrestrained.*

He prowled through the enormous office building until he found the office that was to be Nina's. She had arrived a few hours prior. He decided that he would escort her to the meeting.

The staff meetings were usually held in the late afternoon every Monday. Vasile was older than many of his kind and could be out in early or late sunlight without problem, but it was best if he was seen during daylight hours sometimes.

"Good evening, Miss Caruthers." he addressed her, entering her office.

"Mr. Velicescu! It's good to be here, sir," she said breathlessly, shooting to her feet.

Something was not right. Vasile walked around her desk and stopped a foot in front of her. She tilted her head back to look at him and squeezed her eyes closed in pain.

"Nina?" he asked carefully, "What is wrong?"

Forcing her eyes open a half-inch, she tried to smile. "Really, Mr. Velicescu, I'm fine." she lied.

His ebony eyes studied her face. "Why must you tell me things that are not true, little Nina?" he sighed, shaking his head from side to side.

As he pulled her into his arms, she began to tremble.

16

He rubbed her back. Placing a finger under her chin, he tipped her face back and looked into her eyes.

"Tell me?" he whispered, his black eyes boring into her pain filled turquoise pools.

"It's only a little headache," she confessed. "I'm sure it'll go away."

Against her will, it seemed her head drooped to rest on his shoulder. Scanning her thoughts, he could tell that it was *not* a simple little headache but a very *big* headache. He massaged her temples and spoke to her, soothing her in Romanian. Reaching into her mind, he soothed her and gave her the feeling that her headache was gone and that she'd rested her eyes a moment. Vasile gently eased her into her chair. He moved back to the doorway and opened her office door. Once again, he entered.

"Good evening, Miss Caruthers." he said cheerfully, "May I call you Nina?"

"Of course, Mr. Velicescu!" she blushed uncomfortably, apparently fearing she'd been caught napping.

"Shall we attend the staff meeting?" he asked her in his spellbinding voice. "And Nina?" he asked.

Grabbing the portfolio she'd need for the meeting, she stood and preceded him through the door he held open. "Yes, sir?" she asked.

"Call me Vasile, please."

Watching her walk out in front of him, Vasile considered the question of punishing her. Leaving him, it seemed, had brought with it more punishment than he could possibly mete out. It was enough that she would never be allowed to do it again.

* * * *

Later, he couldn't have been more impressed by her as Nina gave her opinions regarding various employee issues during the meeting. Obviously, she'd done her homework. She also showed a clear understanding of matters concerning how he addressed the government and the consumer, as well.

At one point, she stunned everyone by calling him on the carpet. "Mr. Velicescu, you…" she began.

"Vasile," he corrected her. At her blank look he said, "Call me Vasile, please."

Nina released a barely audible breath. "Fine!" she grouched while her new coworkers blanched. With difficulty, he bit back a smile.

"Vasile," she stated.

"Yes?" he inquired very politely, stifling his amusement.

"Your European accent, while very attractive, is alienating the American public every time you open your mouth on television!" she stated. The entire gathering gasped.

"Oh, good lord!" she turned to Vasile, "Is your upper echelon too delicate for this? Just give me my salary for this week, we'll go in the other room, and I'll tell you what I think. Then I'll go wait tables till the next job comes along."

His face split in a grin. "I think you will make a perfect administrative assistant." Vasile couldn't help but wonder how formidable she would be when she recovered the strength lost in her accident.

* * * *

Near the end of her second week, Nina felt she was beginning to understand what her boss expected of her. Vasile Velicescu was still as inscrutable as ever so she didn't even try to understand him. Instead, she decided she'd treat his business as if it was her own and she'd try to advise him accordingly.

With this in mind, Nina was appalled by the document she had spread on her desk in front of her. According to the terms of the contract her employer was slated to sign, ninety-nine percent of all proceeds resulting from the smaller firm's joining with Velicescu Finance would be spoken for. Velicescu Finance would be funding the success of Maitland Savings with barely enough of a return to pay secretarial fees for typing the contract.

It was a good thing that she had postponed the meeting with Maitland Savings. Still, the New Contracts Department manager should have gone over this with her. Now the man was not returning her calls.

Nina snatched up her phone. "Beverly, it's imperative that I speak to Mr. Velicescu immediately."

"Nina? He's in with Maitland Savings right now." Beverly informed her in her placid voice.

Nina gasped. "It's beyond imperative, Bev." Nina insisted. "Please put me through immediately!"

"I'd better not get yelled at for this…" Bev put her through.

"Nina Caruthers, my assistant." he said to the people in his office. "Nina, say hello to Mr. Yardley and Mr. Reynolds from Maitland Savings." Vasile's satin smooth, cultured voice sent chills of awareness up her spine, even on the phone.

"I'd really rather not, sir. May I speak to you privately, please, Mr. Velicescu?" Nina was in no mood for niceties.

"I am in the middle of a meeting right now, Nina." There was an edge to his refined voice now.

"Mr. Velicescu, I would not interrupt if I didn't feel it was necessary." There was a definite edge to her usually soft voice now, too. Angry with Maitland Savings for trying to cheat him, Nina was equally as angry with her boss for not trusting her enough to find out what she wanted.

"I will come to see you when I have finished here, Nina." he snapped at her.

Speaking in Romanian, Nina said, *"Please turn to*

page thirteen, paragraph thirty-six of the Maitland Contract. I had cancelled that meeting and the department head is avoiding me. Don't sign that contract unless you have an emotional attachment to Maitland Savings." She took a deep breath. He didn't say anything so she went on in English. "I expect I'll be gone when you're done. Thanks for everything, Mr. Velicescu." She hung up.

Nina was shaking. She had just quit her job. *What was she thinking?* Folding her arms on her desk, she buried her face in them. She wasn't sure how long she stayed that way but it could only have been five minutes or so.

Her head snapped up when she heard her office door open and close. Vasile Velicescu leaned against it looking as dangerously attractive and enigmatic as always. It just wasn't fair to be that good-looking and have such a sinfully sexy voice. She'd enjoy it for this one last time.

"So, little Nina, we have our first fight, do we?" he purred, his voice flowing over her like warm honey.

"Who won?" she asked, still shaking.

She leaned back in her chair. Reading her thoughts, he could tell that she was terribly upset but trying to act nonchalant about it. He wanted to be angry with her for attempting once again to leave him but somehow he couldn't. She was just too distressed.

"It would seem that we both did, my Nina. What shall we do to make it up?" He moved fluidly across the room to her. He found himself wanting to soothe and comfort her. Taking her hand, Vasile eased her from the chair and pulled her hand under his arm to rest on the crook of his elbow.

"Let us go have a drink together and discuss what has taken place, hmm?" he suggested, his cultured voice seductive. He led her into the hall as he spoke.

"Sir? Mr. Velicescu, you do know that I quit, don't you?" They were passing people in the hall now and heads turned at her words.

"Ah, but Nina, did I not say that you would not go away from me? I need your assistance in my life. Without it, I shall be alone on this earth." His satiny voice wrapped itself around her.

"Mr. Velicescu..." she began.

"Vasile," he countered.

"Vasile," she sighed. She said nothing more as he guided her into the upscale business club next door.

"Vasile," she tried again, "You have many employees whose opinions you trust and value. I'm sure you won't be alone on this earth, sir. I have apparently..." he interrupted her.

"Will you have a glass of wine, Nina?" At her nod, he told the waiter, "Mocri Pinot please and be sure that Anton pours from my private stock," he instructed. Anton would not pour the second glass from Vasile's bottle.

"Sir? Mr. Velicescu, you do know that I quit, don't you?" They were passing people in the hall now and heads turned at her words.

"Ah, but Nina, did I not say that you would not go away from me? I need your assistance in my life. Without it, I shall be alone on this earth." His satiny voice wrapped itself around her.

"Mr. Velicescu..." she began.

"Vasile." he countered.

"Vasile," she sighed. She said nothing more as he guided her into the upscale business club next door.

"Vasile" she tried again, "You have many employees whose opinions you trust and value. I'm sure you won't be alone on this earth, sir. I have apparently..." he interrupted her.

When the waiter left, Nina tried yet again. "I do not engender you with trust and confidence, Sir. This is not a good working relationship for you to have with your assistant. Life is simply too short to spend it with people you don't trust."

"It is my fault, little Nina. I have grown used to having those people surrounding me worrying more for my temper and less for my business. You must give me time to adjust." He was at his most charming and knew that she was weakening.

"Sir..." she waited while the waiter carefully placed a glass of dark red wine in front of each of them. "Sir, this could have cost millions. It would have left us paying for the privilege of saving Maitland Savings and they'd have stocks in our company as well."

Vasile felt absurdly pleased that she'd referred to Velicescu Finance as "our company". He reached over and took her hand, lifting it and turning her palm upward. Placing a warm and lingering kiss in the center of her palm, Vasile looked at her closely.

"I have learned to take better care to listen to you my Nina. I will be pleased to tell you if I disagree but I promise to give each word you say all the weight it deserves. We will be...partners?"

"Mr....Vasile, I'm sure you will succeed without me as you have for years," she countered, pulling her hand back to her wine glass. "As I said, life is short and you should feel confident in your choices. I don't want to spend my life where my contributions have questionable value."

"You must not leave me surrounded by 'yes' people. Perhaps we can find a way to extend your life so it is less short, hmmm?" He reached over and stroked her cheek with one finger. Looking deeply into her eyes, he told her sharply, "You will stay with me Nina, no more talk of leaving me. Do you understand?"

"I'll stay with you, Mr. Velicescu," Nina parroted, with a sigh.

"The wine is Slovenian. Do you like it?" Vasile asked her, taking a sip.

"I like it very much."

The two spoke of wines and recalcitrant department managers until they had both finished their drinks. They discussed Nina's duties as a corporate attorney before her accident. Finally, Vasile escorted her to her office. By this time, the building was nearly deserted. When she stepped inside, he followed her and closed the door behind him, flicking on one dim light.

He caught her by the shoulders and stood looking down at her. "I am pleased that we have made up our fight, Nina. Are you?"

"Yes," she breathed. "Yes, I am."

Slowly, Vasile lowered his mouth to hers and brushed her lips lightly. "The making it up—that is said to be the best part of a fight, is it not?"

"Yes," she whispered.

He caressed her lips with his for another long minute, smoothing his over hers, back and forth. "I have much enjoyed making up this fight with you, Nina Caruthers." He pulled her to him in a brief hug and then, with difficulty, let her go.

Turning, he left her office, closing the door behind him. Following the mental path to her thoughts, he smiled to himself. She had enjoyed making up after the fight too, it seemed. After Vasile returned to his office, he found himself unable to focus on his work.

For a long time, he considered how Nina had felt when he'd ignored her advice. She had been hurt and perhaps demeaned. *Did* he want her for his partner? Could he respect her enough to take her advice more seriously?

Chapter Three

A week later, Vasile awoke disconcerted. Something had brought him awake a little before his usual time and he wasn't sure what it was. He searched his mind for a minute until it came to him. Instantly, he was alert.

Nina was in fear. Something had frightened her so badly that she was almost crying. Where was she? He connected with her enough to see that she was in her office. What could scare her in his office building? Her safety should be certain there.

In minutes, he entered the building. Mentally he scanned her surroundings as he made his way toward her. No aggressors seemed to be present. There was no violence that he could locate.

As he passed two men chatting in a doorway, he heard one man say he didn't know if Nina would be present at the meeting that afternoon. This concerned Vasile a great deal. He quietly entered her office and found her at her desk sobbing into her folded arms.

Vasile moved in front of her and pulled her against his chest. She remained encircled in his arms while he soothed her and murmured in Romanian to her. He noticed that she felt very hot to the touch.

"I'm sorry, sir," she finally apologized. "I don't know what's come over me. I've tried to stop. I just don't know what's wrong." She struggled to contain the tears but they still fell from her eyes. She seemed so weak to him.

"Hush, *meu dragoste,*" he whispered to her, calling her *my love*. "I am here now." Vasile leaned down and kissed her falling tears. "Are you unwell, little Nina?" he asked her.

"Sir?" she questioned him. He'd learned that this was her way of avoiding answering his questions.

He focused his unrelenting stare on her and commanded her, "Nina, you must tell me. Do you feel ill?"

He already knew that she didn't want to answer. He was still surprised when, with some difficulty, she managed to turn her head away.

Placing one finger under her chin, Vasile brought her face back to his. He could feel her mental and physical struggle. He was impressed by her ability to resist him at all. The small amount of strength she'd found to defy him was ebbing away. Tears fell harder now.

"Now, little Nina, you *will* tell me, are you ill?" his voice brooked no argument. She had to answer him.

"Yes, I have a fever." Her chin trembled.

"Is that what you fear, *meu dragoste*? You are afraid your body will not heal?" he asked her kindly.

"Yes," she whispered. "I want to be here with you. No more hospitals," she sniffed.

Still holding her chin by a finger, he looked at her thoughtfully for long moments. He unbuttoned his suit coat and slipped it off, waved at the door, locking it. He threaded his hand into her hair and drew her against him. Tilting her head back, his gaze burned into hers until her heavy lids slowly closed.

He lifted her, gathered her to his chest, and sat down on the sofa with her in his lap. With one hand, he removed his tie and unbuttoned his silk shirt. Taking two fingers, he embedded his nails in the flesh over his heart and sliced a little opening in the vein.

When the blood began to trickle from his small cut, he placed her lips over it and sent her the urge to open her mouth. He held her head in place with one hand so that the blood would drip onto her tongue.

"Swallow it, *meu dragoste*," Vasile encouraged her. "Take more into your mouth, Nina," his black satin voice ordered. Even in his thrall, she resisted a little. He

25

kissed her temple and told her again, "Drink from me, *meu dragoste*, only a little to help fight the infection."

He felt the tip of her hot tongue trace the small cut above his breast. Need slammed into his body in a solid wave. He hardened and tightened instantly. She whimpered in protest and he breathed words of comfort into her ear. He sent another, stronger mental command that she suck the blood into her mouth. She began to suck lightly. He stopped her after a short time and held her against him, letting her rest.

As he cradled her on his lap, he pulled out his cell phone. "Beverly, I am running late today. Push the staff meeting back an hour. I will tell Miss Caruthers of the change since I must go over some things with her prior to the meeting." He hung up the phone without waiting for a response.

Vasile studied Nina's sleeping features. She'd lost a great deal of weight and she'd never had any to spare, in his opinion. As his eyes roamed over her pale face, he noted the deep purple bruises of fatigue under her eyes. He also saw a long, thin scar that disappeared into her hairline beginning above one cheekbone.

He thought back to the pain he'd felt that evening two years ago before he'd ceased to feel her. When she'd described her injuries, he'd imagined her broken body pinned in the filthy mud.

Now, he explored her memories of the accident and once again saw her elderly grandmother wrenched from her arms and crushed by the train car. He felt with her those terrible moments when she'd flown through the air and tried to protect herself from the falling debris. Guiltily he searched her mind and found that, as she'd watched certain death hurtle toward her, her last thoughts had been of him.

He remembered, two years ago, hearing her scream in his mind, *Please, forgive me. If I'd had one more minute to live, I'd live it with you!* and then she was gone.

She had once again come close to dying. Was she destined to die a painful, horrible death? Was she destined to die before her time?

Not if he could help it!

He'd give her a month or two longer to get to know him but he would claim her for his mate soon after that. Vasile thought about that a minute. *His mate...*

Vasile hadn't realized consciously that he'd intended to make her his mate. He knew he wasn't going to let her go again. Making her his mate was the only logical next step.

He'd fed on her blood many times while he'd been buried inside her body. She wouldn't be his mate until she took his blood at the same time. They must drink from each other while joined. He could probably compel her to exchange blood with him. He could, but it would be so much better if she made the choice for herself.

Carefully, Vasile lifted her and placed her back at her desk with her head resting on her folded arms. He straightened his clothing and replaced his tie. Pulling his suit jacket back on, he sent her the mental nudge that would wake her up. He unlocked her office door and appeared to be entering when she lifted her head.

She seemed flustered and disoriented. She pulled a small compact out and tried to assess the damages of smudged eyeliner and lip color.

"I'm so sorry, Mr. Velicescu, Vasile, I mean. I must have rested my head and…"

"Do not worry, *meu dragoste*, you are in no trouble with me." He walked to her and took her face in his hands. "You look beautiful, Nina, as you always do."

"Sir? Mr. Velicescu? I mean, Vasile." She went red in the face. He could tell that she was still flustered. "I'm not very lovable *or* beautiful." She blushed, looking uneasy.

"Nonsense!"   he   declared.

He'd called her "my love" and possibly she wondered at that. He hadn't remembered that she understood his language.

"Romanians, we are sentimental. Please, Nina, I am sure the anticipation of our weekly staff meeting has overwhelmed you with excitement therefore causing your exhaustion." His ebony eyes twinkled at her. "Let us join the meeting and address this week's crisis," he told her, wrapping an arm around her shoulders.

Obviously, she didn't know what to make of his familiarity but she didn't struggle with him. Part of him wanted to walk into the meeting with her in his arms. No man would dare to touch her if they knew she belonged to him. As they walked toward the conference room, he told her what he planned to cover in the meeting. With difficulty, he moved away from her when they joined the group already assembled.

* * * *

After ten that night, Nina was finalizing a response to an overseas client regarding the new China Banking Regulatory Commission and Velicescu Finance. Since she was beginning to fight the fever again, she tried even harder to focus on the task at hand. She was so engrossed in her work that Vasile's phone call surprised her.

"Nina, may I speak with you, please? Come to my office." There were many people still working even as late at night as it was so it took her a few minutes to get there. Knowing she was his assistant, a "yes" or "no" from Nina was almost as good as a "yes" or "no" from Vasile.

Entering his office, she spoke up immediately, "I'm sorry, sir, three people stopped me on the way in. They all had life or death…"

Vasile walked up to her and placed his hand on her forehead. "How are you feeling, little Nina?" Her skin still felt warmer than it should.

"Excuse me, sir? I'm ..." she began, somewhat startled.

His black eyes bored into her turquoise ones. "Nina?" he said very softly. "Answer me."

She began to tremble. "I feel fine," she whispered.

His onyx gaze held her prisoner. "Nina, you will tell me no fiction." His voice was a satin whip demanding an honest answer.

"A little lightheaded but better." she whispered in a low voice. "Please don't fire me, Mr. ... Vasile." she began to shake harder now.

Would he yell at her? Would he fire her? He had a reputation as a rigid man who wanted his staff to be sharp and ready to work. She couldn't have been more surprised when he reached out one hand and cupped her cheek.

"Nina, it is permissible, is it not, to leave work early when one is feeling poorly?" he asked her. "I offer each of my employees what is known as 'sick days', do I not?"

"Y-Y-yes, S-s-s-sir," she stuttered.

"I'm sure this qualifies as an incidence when you are justified in leaving work before your scheduled time, *Da*?" he asked reasonably.

"I guess so, S-s–sir," she finally responded.

"Nina?" he caressed her cheekbone with his thumb. "When you climb into your bed tonight and close your eyes, please to do something for me?" his sensual, seductive voice stroked her senses.

"Okay." She stared at him wide eyed.

"Please to say my name over and over again until you fall asleep, hmmm, little Nina? Perhaps then you will get used to calling me Vasile instead of Mr. Velicescu."

Chapter Four

Around eleven-thirty that night, Vasile found himself at a crowded bar. He stood just outside the door watching the arriving clientele. When a group of healthy young men came toward him laughing, he joined them. Soon two of them walked around the building with him, determined to bet on the outcome of the football game they'd come to watch.

He fed from the first man and then leaned him against the building. Taking the other man, he stretched an arm across his shoulders and leaned in as if he were confiding a secret. He fed well from both men.

When he was finished, he implanted the idea that one man had called the correct points spread and the other the correct number of yards gained by his favorite team. They would believe that they'd scuffled briefly with fans from the opposing team, explaining their fatigue and soreness. He tucked a hundred dollar bill inside each man's pocket to be discovered at just the right time and took his leave of the bar.

With his hunger satisfied, Vasile turned his mind more fully to Nina. He had been constantly touching her mind gently to assure himself that she was okay. She'd done some of what he'd instructed. In her mind, she'd repeated his name every so often.

Over the span of the last hour, though, Nina had seemed less and less lucid. Now he found that she was shaking with chills and barely coherent.

He'd been to her new house since she'd come to work as his assistant, but she hadn't invited him in and he'd never asked to enter. Tapping softly on the door, Vasile sent her the message that it was okay to answer.

The door swung open and Nina stood in the doorway wearing a long, white linen gown that buttoned up the front and was gathered at the wrists. It had little pink flowers embroidered near the scooped collar. She looked young and innocent in her bare feet, and painfully delicate.

"Vasile? Have you come to visit me?" she asked. She seemed dazed, her face flushed. "Please come in, you'll catch a cold." Nina stepped back from the door and would have crumpled to the floor if he hadn't caught her.

"Nina, my Nina," he admonished her, holding her body against his chest. "What have you done to yourself?"

"I forgot to fill my medicine," she confessed into his neck.

He pressed a kiss to her hot forehead and rubbed his cheek against hers.

"What will I do if you die again, *meu dragoste*?" he murmured into her hair.

"Vasile, I was watching a movie. I can't die till it's over. Will you watch it with me?" she implored him. "I don't want to go to bed yet."

"*Da* little Nina, we will watch your movie. But you must do something for me, hmm?" He carried her into the living room where her television was showing *"Willy Wonka and the Chocolate Factory"*.

"Shall I make you some popcorn?" she offered in a murmur.

He chuckled at her, laying her down among the nest of sheets and blankets she'd laid on her couch.

"No popcorn, *meu dragoste*." he assured her, kicking his shoes off and removing his jacket and shirt. "I will need a kiss goodnight before you sleep. Right here, okay?" he pointed at the place on his neck just below his jaw where his carotid artery was pulsing strongly.

"*Da*, Nina?" he asked her.

"*Da*" she responded.

31

He slid behind her, pulling her onto his lap, and held her as they watched the Oompa Loompas sing their final song. He usually didn't watch movies or television. Laughing, he found himself wondering how much of this was getting through to her in her fevered state.

"Its true." she answered his unspoken question. "If you're not greedy, you *should* go far. I love the Oompa Loompas. I want to live in happiness as they do. I wouldn't even mind being orange with green hair." Nina offered Vasile a beatific smile.

He kissed her forehead and stretched the two of them out on her sofa. She didn't fall asleep but he felt her mind fading in and out. He chuckled to himself.

My beautiful Nina with orange skin and green hair… I hope she doesn't have a secret fondness for those clothes…

He felt her mind begin to drift off to sleep. He turned her body toward his on the wide couch and tilted her face to his.

"I can't see the movie, Vasile," she mumbled in sleepy complaint.

"Shh, *meu dragoste*, I will tell you what happens." he promised her. "Look into my eyes, Nina."

She forced her eyes open. "Vasile? Please leave the TV on and let me stay here when you go, okay?"

He nodded. "You will open your mouth on my neck, Nina. You will swallow the blood when it flows."

His black eyes fixed on her smoky cyan colored eyes, compelling her. He saw her confusion for only a second and then she breathed, "Okay, Vasile, if that's what you want."

He slid his fingers into her hair and held her head in the palm of his hand. With his free hand, he reached over and made a small hole in the artery using his fingernail. Quickly, he placed her mouth over the spurting blood. He made sure her mouth was opened and blood trickled in.

He felt himself grow hard as her lips and tongue

32

moved on his neck. The sensation of her lapping at the tiny wound made him desperate for more of her. He slid his hand under the hem of her gown and up her legs, finding her nakedness.

She never wore undergarments to bed. He'd destroyed three or four pair of panties that first year before she got the message. She was still prepared for him to come to her. Moving his hand between her legs, he found her wet and very ready for him.

"Ahhh, my Midnight Guardian," she breathed when he touched her feminine heat. He pressed her mouth back to the trickling blood.

His voice was strangled as he said, "Drink, *meu dragoste.*"

He wanted to thrust himself inside of her. He wanted to bury his fangs in her pounding pulse. He could barely contain himself his hunger was so ravenous for her.

"I want…" she whispered. "Please?"

"Shh, little Nina," he whispered back to her.

Vasile moved his fingers back and forth through her wetness and eased one finger inside of her. He knew she'd been celibate these last two years.

"Yes." Against his throat, he felt her release a soft sigh.

"Drink" he said pulling his hand away from her center.

She began sucking at the small puncture again. He slowly eased two fingers back into her and felt her arm slip around his waist.

He heard her mind weeping, "*I thought you'd never come back to me.*" She continued to suck at the cut over his artery.

"*As long as you live, I will be with you,*" he thought to her in return.

"*I've missed you so much,*" her mind whispered.

"I've missed you just as much, *meu inimã,*" he murmured to her aloud. Would she know that he'd spoken? Would she know that he called her his heart? He realized that, if he had one, she was exactly that.

The fingers cupping her rounded bottom flexed and he could tell that she was no longer feverish. Her body temperature was normal. He withdrew the fingers between her legs.

She mewled in protest and he reached up and closed the wound at his throat. Her eyes were open and she looked at him as if she might cry. He moved his hand back between her legs. Pressing her clit with his thumb, he continued to plunge a finger in and out of her, soon adding a second one. He opened his pants and freed his rigid erection.

Then he pulled his hand away from her wet heat and moved his swollen shaft between her legs positioning it beneath her moist labia. He rubbed her with the tip of his rod until he could stand no more and slid it between her legs.

He would not put himself inside of her but instead he rubbed her nub and her wet lips back and forth over his hard erection. At the same time, he moved to plunge his two fingers into her from behind. When he felt his climax building, he sank his fangs into the pulse at her neck.

Vasile growled his climax as she screamed hers. Careful not to drink more than she could stand, he fed only enough to satisfy the worst of his hunger for her. He licked the tiny holes closed and held her in his arms for a long time.

He'd never get enough of her. Her blood was the finest wine to him. Her body was so welcoming, so perfect. He realized that Nina was his home, his heart. He had to keep her in his life.

Entering her mind again, he reinforced that she'd had an erotic dream about him where her old lover and he became the same man. He knew that she had had strong feelings for him when he was little more than a sexual phantom to her. He believed that she was developing real feelings for

34

him now.

He could only send her desires in the direction they wished to go anyway. Still, he reinforced the joining of his old self with the man she knew today. He'd learn soon how successful he'd been.

Carefully, he moved her so that she was facing the television again and he sat looking down at her. He saw that her black wavy hair had grown long again. It brushed the top of her shoulders now. Soon it would be as long as it had been two years ago.

Her delicate face was so pale. Her full lips were so pink and beckoning. She was his beautiful Snow White. Vasile instructed her mentally to call in sick the next day.

* * * *

When Nina awoke the next afternoon, she was already very late for work. In a panic, she called Beverly.

"Oh Nina," cooed Beverly, "You really have to talk to Mr. Velicescu. Hang on, let me transfer you…"

"Wait, Bev, what kind of a mood is he in?" Nina asked hurriedly.

"Hmmm, Nina Caruthers, what kind of a mood would you like him to be in?" purred the black satin and velvet voice she'd been dreaming about.

"Vasile," she whispered breathlessly. She was sure she must sound like she had sex on her mind.

"Beautiful Nina, you keep me in that kind of a mood, did you not know?" His caressing, seductive voice vibrated down the phone to her.

"Um, Sir? I'm sorry but I overslept and…" she couldn't seem to string one coherent thought together just now.

"Hush, little Nina," he crooned. "Stay home today, hmmm? I will check on you later, *Da*?"

"Thank you… Thank you, Vasile." she was so embarrassed.

"Do not worry, Nina. Stay home and recuperate.

35

Watch a movie. Perhaps you can go to bed early. You are welcome to dream you are with me instead of coming to work."

She heard him chuckling at her as she hung up the phone. Since she didn't know how to take his smug male amusement, she chose to ignore it.

Nina didn't feel ill anymore. She felt pretty good, really. *Okay, the truth was that she felt better than she had the day before. In all honesty, that didn't really qualify as "pretty good."*

For a little while, she stayed nestled in her bed just thinking about her boss and the amazing dream she'd had about him. She'd dreamed that she'd finally seen her Midnight Guardian's face. It had been Vasile.

They'd watched a movie and then he'd made love with her. She also dreamed they had taken blood from each other. She wasn't sure where the Oompa Loompas had come in but she had a memory of them as well.

Nina was more than a little embarrassed about how attracted she was to Vasile Velicescu. In fact, she was worried about how she felt. He was dark and well built. He did remind her of her Midnight Guardian in that way.

Nina remembered the first time her Midnight Guardian had made love to her. She remembered it with Vasile Velicescu's face.

She'd fallen asleep wearing only her robe. She'd awakened to find him kissing her. His touch was so gentle and loving. He'd slowly taken her hands and placed them on his chest. He'd untied her robe and opened it. He'd then kissed and touched every bit of her. He'd suckled her breasts and fondled her nipples. He'd rubbed her clit and penetrated her with his fingers making her come again and again. When she was so overwhelmed with her many climaxes that she didn't think she could even feel excitement again, he had raised himself above her.

Lowering his mouth to hers, he'd slowly entered her wet channel. His cock had pushed its way through her dripping folds until he was buried deep inside her. He gave her a little time to get used to the feeling.

She had been completely overwhelmed. Slowly at first, he began pumping himself into her. He'd plunged into her body over and over. She began coming almost right away and didn't stop until after he climaxed. He then kissed her tears away and held her in his arms. He let her doze a while and then awakened her.

Once again, he'd parted her legs and licked her labia, her clit, her little opening. He sucked her and plunged his tongue into her. He moved her to her tummy and entered her from behind. As he plunged into her she'd thrust back against him.

She would never forget the ecstasy of that night. If only he would have spoken to her. When she moved to speak to him, he'd placed his fingers on her lips, shaking his head. She realized then that theirs was to be a silent exchange. Their only language would be passion.

Now, thinking of it, it was so easy to replace Vasile's face and body with the dark shadow that had been her Midnight Guardian. She'd kept track of every minute she'd spent with him in her little diary. He wasn't Vasile and she couldn't let herself imagine that he was. What kind of a fool was she if she fell for her boss? She was turning into a lonely old spinster.

She pulled out some of her favorite movies, *Young Frankenstein, Princess Bride, Ever After* and had a little movie festival. Around one in the morning, she cleaned up her movie litter and made her way to bed.

* * * *

A little past two in the morning, Vasile prowled around the office, reached for Nina's mind and found her sleeping. He continued looking into her subconscious and was surprised to find an indistinct memory of himself flitting through her thoughts.

She was worried about falling for him and the trouble that could cause. *She was attracted to him, but also felt nervous and insecure.*

Nina wanted him. She also wanted the man she remembered. His body tightened. He was hungry for her in every way. He made his way to her townhouse. As he entered, he could hear her restlessness and tossing in her bed. He knew he could come to her as the lover he used to be, but now he wanted more.

Vasile sat on the bed and reached for her. "Nina, *meu dragoste,* come to me," he bade her, peeling off his shirt and kicking off his shoes.

She didn't open her eyes but she rolled toward him. He brushed back the sheet and comforter that covered her. Her eyes opened and she was seeing him as if in a dream.

She wore a long sleeved, pink satin sleep shirt that brushed the tops of her thighs. His body was hard and heavy. He reached for the hem of her short gown and caught the bottom with one finger. He edged it up an inch and saw the tiny black curls peeking out at the vee of her thighs.

Vasile reinforced in her mind the idea that she was dreaming. He slid into bed facing her and trailed his hand up her thigh. With one hand, he sliced a small cut into the heavy artery over his heart. He pressed her lips to it. Her sleeping mind was easily manipulated. She began to suck. He slid his fingers into the nest of curls covering her womanly treasure. She moaned, arching her hips toward him.

Unzipping his pants, he pulled his heavy erection free. He raised her leg over his and slid into her warmth. His fangs lengthened in his mouth. He slowly moved in and out of her, cupping her bottom in his hands. He wanted to thrust hard. He could make her his mate this very minute if he fed from her now.

He knew they would come at the same time. Her juices and his would mingle. Her blood and his would be pulsing through both their bodies. She was his—she belonged to him. He was nearly overwhelmed with the intense need to guarantee that she would be his for all time.

He knew he had to let her make the choice to change of her own free will. If he didn't, she would never be happy. Her happiness was so important to him.

Reluctantly, he pulled his still rigid cock from her body, tucking it back into his pants. When he joined with Nina again, he wanted her to know he was making love with her. She reached for him. He closed the wound on his breast. Until then, he would try to ease his hunger for her and meet her needs at the same time.

He lowered his mouth to hers and eased his hand between her legs until he once again found her silk heat covered by tiny curls. With his thumb, he massaged her little nub and he gently pumped two fingers into her rhythmically. When she was close to her climax, he reached behind her with his other hand and pressed the tip of his finger into her puckered little opening. At the same time, he sunk his fangs into the pulse at her throat.

She tightened on both his hands and sobbed out her climax, burying her fingernails into his back. Moaning, Vasile felt himself come in his pants. Slowly, he withdrew his finger from her nether hole and his other hand from between her legs. He eased her nightgown back down her legs, then licked the pinpricks on her neck closed.

He stared into her eyes and sent her a command to sleep and remember this as another dream she had of making love to her boss. He wanted her to remember the blood exchange in her dream. He wanted her subconscious to accept, even desire, the drinking of each other's blood.

Chapter Five

The next day, Vasile was looking for Nina when he noticed several people filing out of a small conference room just down the hall from her office. He heard Nina's voice joined with that of another man. She was talking to Soames, the manager from the Consumer Loan division.

Deciding to eavesdrop, he seated himself in a waiting area nearby and listened.

"Well Miss Caruthers, I'd say you've achieved a great deal since you've joined our little family."

"Why, thank you Mr. Soames, I enjoy being here," Nina responded. Vasile smiled.

"What part of being here do you enjoy the most? Let me put that another way. Which one of your duties is more strenuous?" Mr. Soames asked.

"I'm afraid I'm not sure what you're asking, Mr. Soames." Vasile noticed a warning edge to her voice now.

"What's more difficult, Miss Caruthers, leading the project team or fucking the boss?" Vasile felt his fangs burst in his mouth. "Did you know that we call him Drac?" Soames asked.

Vasile shot to his feet but her next words stopped him. He forced himself to follow her mental path and see what she was seeing.

"I'd say fucking the boss is *harder*, Mr. Soames." Her husky laugh floated through the air. "Forgive me, Mr. Soames, I couldn't resist. Seriously, it does bring with it all kinds of extra responsibilities. You should pay attention here." Her voice was firmer now. Vasile wished he could see her face but her anger was coming through loud and clear.

He heard her shift and could tell that she was leaning closer to the man. He couldn't control a growl. He hoped she didn't hear it. He knew she'd associate it with her phantom lover's anger.

"Since fucking the boss is a singular talent of mine and goes above and beyond my stated responsibilities, I expect to be amply compensated. You understand that means I keep my eye on the prize?"

Mr. Soames could be heard moving. Looking through Nina's eyes, Vasile saw the man nodding his head. It was obvious he hadn't expected this reaction from Nina.

"With that in mind, it would behoove you to remember that I guard each and every one of Mr. Velicescu's interests like a jealous wife." Soames swallowed loudly and nodded again. "That said, I've noticed that your department is not going to feather my nest this quarter." She paused. "I don't like that." He heard the sound of a chair rolling back. He could tell she was moving.

"I had my eye on a little trinket, Mr. Soames, but the projected earnings have suffered. And Mr. Velicescu promised to donate to my favorite charity, but today, loan reports were down."

She had paced away from the man. Now she turned back to lean inches from his face. "Because of you, I don't get my little treats." Her eyes seemed to narrow. "I don't think I'll suck his dick tonight, Mr. Soames." Vasile jerked. He heard and saw her move around the table. "If Ol' Drac is cranky in the morning, I'd lock myself in my office if I were you."

Nina nearly plowed into Vasile in the hallway. She obviously wondered what he'd heard. She mumbled something about the Humane Society and fled toward the elevators. *Her favorite charity?*

Vasile ambled to the conference room she'd just left.

"Soames, is it?" he inquired of the man still seated at the table, shaking nervously. "I thought Nina was meeting with some people in here? We are…we will be getting together later, I think. I thought I could confirm that." Vasile gave Soames a man-to-man smile and left.

The next day, Vasile made a point of seeking Soames out. He scorched his ears about the failings of his department and how that someone would be replaced. He gave a credible impression of a man whose dick did *not* get sucked the previous evening.

Since the idea of Nina taking his cock in her mouth had made him hungrier for her than he already was, Vasile didn't mind making someone pay.

* * * *

Nina decided that she was becoming too infatuated with her boss. *Two wet dreams in a row? Okay, ten wet dreams in a row...*

She resolved that she needed to get out or something. It just wasn't a good idea to have such a monster crush on the man she worked for like this. It would be bad enough if she didn't work so closely with him but she was his administrative assistant. He would never be attracted to someone like her, she was sure of that. No good could come of this.

Physically, Nina was feeling better these days than she had in so long. One weekend evening, she agreed to meet some of the department managers from the project team for a drink. She felt a little like a fifth wheel at first but she made herself stay at the bar. Several people showed up that she hadn't expected to see. Soon, a kind of "party" atmosphere permeated the group.

"Sometimes ol' Drac joins us when we show up here!" one of the women said in a conspiratorial whisper.

"He does?" Nina was surprised. It was a nice bar but she just didn't think of Vasile as a 'bar' kind of guy. "I'm sure he wouldn't want to run into me on his day off!" she laughed. "I know he gets tired of my ugly mug!"

One of the guys grabbed her and demanded, "Okay,

who's been slipping Nina doubles? She's obviously drunk over here!"

Everybody laughed but Nina felt a little funny. "Don't worry about Michael," Wanda from Business Loans had soothed her. "He likes to be the center of attention. So, Nina, tell us *all* about Mr. Velicescu!"

"Yeah, Nina, how do you like staring at *that* 'ugly mug' all day?" Jeanne, one of the secretaries laughed.

"Be honest, Nina! You know you think he's hot!" Jeannie's best friend Gail piped up.

She knew her face was crimson. "Umm," she began, not sure what to say. "Maybe just a little warm…"

"Warm?" gasped Jeanne, "He's smokin'!"

"Tell us a little secret about him, Nina. Just a tiny one," Wanda begged.

Nina took a deep breath. *Oh hell! Life is short.* "Don't get me in trouble you guys!" she warned.

"Oh, no!" protested Gail.

"Of course not!" Wanda shook her head solemnly.

"Well, he's a closet *Brak* fan." She paused for effect. "He likes to watch it at eleven on Tuesday nights with a big bowl of *Peanut Butter Captain Crunch™*. He likes *Space Ghost*, too."

Everybody got quiet. Nina wasn't sure what to do. Were they astounded? Angry?

"You promised never to tell my secret, Nina."

No! Only one man on the planet had such a warm, sexy, midnight bedroom voice.

Slowly, she turned toward Vasile. *Why does the floor never open up when you need it to?*

"Fancy meeting you here, Vasile," she croaked.

"Ahh, but I had to come, Nina. It was only a matter of time before you revealed my secret fetish for marshmallow chickens."

Nina breathed a sigh of relief. She could see his lips

43

twitch in a barely contained smile. He slid onto a high stool someone had vacated next to her and leaned in close.

"You must tell me all about this '*Brak*' so that I recognize the memorabilia when my employees begin plying me with it. Lucky for you, my Nina, I happen to like *Peanut Butter Captain Crunch™*." He slid an arm around her shoulders and gave her a squeeze.

No guts, no glory, I guess. "Does that mean I have to eat all the marshmallow chickens you end up with?" She knew her face was as red as his wine.

"I think our Nina requires a glass of wine—and a shot of whiskey!" he called out. "It does indeed. Wretched things aren't they?" he chuckled.

Later that night, snug in her bed, Nina admitted that she was doomed. It was bad enough that Vasile Velicescu was sexy, handsome, smelled good, and had that black velvet voice with the old world accent. To find out that he was both fun and funny – how was a girl supposed to fight those odds?

Chapter Six

When one of the lawyers who had offices in their building asked Nina to go to a concert with him the next week, desperately she accepted. She had to do something to combat this head over heels like, lust, crush she had for her boss before it became love.

It was to be a casual date but she was looking forward to it. The singer was one of her favorites who specialized in a Jazz, Blues, and Rock 'n Roll blend of music.

Nervously, Nina broached the subject of the night off with Vasile.

"Vasile, would you mind if I left really early on Friday?" she asked him that Tuesday morning before going home.

"Is anything pressing that evening?" he asked her smoothly. His cultured, old European accent sent chills of awareness up her spine. She was in so much trouble with this man.

"No, Sir. All's quiet on the banking front," she told him.

She was standing near his shoulder having just gone over a series of documents with him. He turned toward her and she was nearly standing between his knees. *I could be in his lap if there was a wrinkle in this carpet. Damn that plastic chair mat!*

"You are not ill again are you, Nina?" he asked her.

"Oh no, Sir," she responded quickly. "I'm going to a music performance with Jack Gibson from the law firm. I'm really looking forward to it." Nina smiled broadly at Vasile. *Yep, really looking forward to it. Really.*

* * * *

Vasile felt something he hadn't felt in a long time— uncertainty. His stomach dropped and he wondered if

45

Nina preferred the company of this human to his company. Frowning, he studied her face. Tilting his head and pursing his lips, he considered her for a moment.

"So you are dating a lawyer, little Nina? Do you like him?" Vasile asked her, looking deeply into her eyes.

"Um, I wouldn't say dating, Sir. I hardly know him." She smiled. "I just like the music and he asked me to go."

"No other reason, little Nina?" he purred.

She looked down and turned her face away from him. That was all he needed. She didn't want him to see how she felt. Just knowing that she had accepted a date with another man to run from her feelings for him was a mixed blessing. While the idea of her being alone with any other man made him furious, he managed to calm himself. It wasn't as if he would actually let her go out with this lawyer, Jack Gibson.

* * * *

On Wednesday, Nina got a call from Jack Gibson, canceling their date. He told her, honestly, that there was someone else that he really had to take to the show. She was disappointed, not because she wouldn't be seeing Jack, but because she really liked the singer performing.

By that time, Vasile and Nina had achieved a comfortable working relationship. Many nights they worked together until the only staff in the building were the security guards.

Vasile would not let her stay as late as he did. Some days he stayed until eight in the morning. Her day ended at one in the morning. More than once, he insisted she finish any instructions for her staff and let him drive her home.

When he did drive her home, Nina felt compelled to invite him in. He was, after all, doing her a favor. Usually, Vasile declined but Thursday morning after he drove her home early in the morning, he accepted. She was only a little nervous – she knew he wouldn't hurt her.

She welcomed him in and offered him a drink or a

bite to eat. He looked at her oddly, as she kicked her shoes off and nudged them toward the wall by the door.

"It's a habit, I guess." She smiled to him. Just as she spoke, a tiny gray animal shot into the room and launched itself at her. It landed on her hip before it began to hiss at Vasile. He reached out and tilted its little face up and stroked it, staring intently at the pintsized beast.

"What is her name?" he asked Nina, peeling it from her hip.

"Abby" she grinned in delight. "It's for how much I love her. Absolutely."

He chuckled, handing the kitten back to her. "I wanted to speak with you, Nina, away from the office," he said finally.

She was instantly nervous. He slipped a palm under her elbow and guided her to her couch, and took a chair across from her.

Looking at her face, he said, "I heard you telling Beverly that Mr. Jack Gibson cancelled your date."

"Yes, he did, Vasile," she told him. "I guess I won't need to leave early that day after all."

"Nina, I would like you to come with me to this event," he said. "I would very much like to have a date with you."

She was sure she was looking at him as if he had three heads. *Date? Vasile Velicescu wanted to take her on a date? Plain Jane Nina Caruthers on a date with Vasile Velicescu?*

"Me?" she croaked.

He chuckled. "You, Nina" he said. "I will come here and get you at seven on Friday?" He raised a sleek brow at her in question.

"Yes, please, Vasile, I'd like to come with you." She could have clapped her hands over her mouth as soon as she heard herself utter the words. *How needy had that sounded?*

"You will accompany me as my lovely companion

whose friendship and intelligence I enjoy?" his eyes wrapped her in black satin and his voice felt like velvet stroking over her.

"Yes, as a companion and not an employee," she said with a slight smile.

Vasile walked to her, and leaning down, kissed her forehead. "Thank you, Nina. I am looking most forward to this."

He left shortly after that. Nina was agog. Vasile Velicescu had requested the pleasure of her company... She was more excited about spending an evening with Vasile than she was about seeing her favorite performer.

* * * *

Vasile was still smiling to himself when he stopped to feed on the way back to the office. He chose a restaurant worker taking a break from busing tables. When he'd satisfied himself, he'd tucked a couple of hundred dollar bills into the man's pocket. He implanted the memory of finding the money after hitting his head and falling.

It made him smile to realize that Nina didn't know how beautiful she was. She didn't understand that all men most likely found her irresistible and he was no exception. The idea of other men wanting her didn't sit too well with him but he'd try to control himself for now. He wanted her to know him for himself and not just as her boss.

When she'd kicked her shoes to the wall, he'd been overcome by the memory of the last time he'd had sexual relations with her. His mind drifted back to his last night with her before she took that fateful trip.

As she had entered her home, she kicked off first one shoe and then its mate, pushing them to the wall by the door. He'd been waiting for her. She turned to flick on the light when his arms came around her.

Vasile slid one hand under her short blouse, palming her breast while the other hand skimmed her abdomen.

48

He kissed her neck and pulled the blouse off her shoulder with his teeth.

His hand on Nina's abdomen slipped lower, into her panties. A finger found its way between the folds of her sex. Her knees began to buckle but he held her firmly. Still holding her from behind, he pulled his hands from under her clothes. He unbuttoned her blouse and tugged it off, removing her bra just as efficiently.

Quickly, Vasile unsnapped and unzipped her jeans pushing them down her legs, lifting her to remove them the rest of the way. When she was completely naked, he renewed his onslaught on her body.

Standing behind her, he plunged two fingers inside of her while he massaged her breasts with his other hand. He nipped at her neck and the back of her shoulder, sucking out a little blood each time and licking the puncture wounds closed.

When he decided she was ready, he lowered her to her knees and unfastened his own pants. He fell to his knees, held her hips in his hands, and entered her from behind. As his cock slid deeply inside of her, Vasile sunk his teeth into the pulse at her neck and shoulder and fed. He thrust again and again, harder and more deeply each time.

Suddenly, he pulled out. She whimpered in complaint.

"Shhh" he whispered.

He rolled her to her back, kissed her, and caressed her while removing his black shirt and jeans. When his naked form rose above her, he leaned down and kissed her deeply. He slid down her body, massaging her breasts with both hands. He began kissing her abdomen and then lower still. When he got to her sex, he spread her legs apart with his hands.

Lowering his face to her sex, he began licking her and making love to her with his tongue. Alternating between drinking her juices and sucking her clit, he soon had her writhing on the floor.

He clamped each hand on one of her thighs and held her still. When he felt her begin to climax, he buried his long incisors into the flesh on either side of her clit. He drank for a moment until her climax subsided. With a flick of his tongue, he closed the wounds.

Lifting her, he carried her down the hall, gently laying her on the bed. He covered her with his body and slid his cock into her. Slowly, lovingly, he pumped himself into her until he could hold back no more.

His cock lengthened and widened, then shot hot semen into her. She screamed out hoarsely when she climaxed. He, too, shouted as he lowered his mouth to her breast, suckled and drank while they came together.

He cuddled her and kissed her until she fell asleep. Stretched out beside her, he leaned over her and looked down at her face. She was so beautiful to him. Her long, wavy black hair fell almost to her elbow. How he loved seeing it spread over the white pillowcases.

He knew she had enjoyed his lovemaking…He thought she still did. Vasile didn't like the direction these thoughts were going. He decided instead to focus on the upcoming "date" he would have with Nina.

Chapter Seven

Nina was trying valiantly to contain her excitement when Vasile arrived to pick her up on Friday evening. She was wearing a close fitting, embroidered denim dress with long sleeves. It had a straight skirt and she wore light slippers with it and no stockings.

Vasile nodded in approval as he helped her into his Jaguar. Experiencing a sense of déjà vu, her eyes drank in the sight of him in black denim jeans and a snug black shirt.

"So, little Nina," he said, taking her hand, "what shall we discuss on our way to this concert? I can now extol the virtues of the baloney sandwich or, if you prefer, I have learned an entertaining song about beans."

Nina had to grin. Apparently, his employees were torturing Vasile with Brak songs and sayings from the Space Ghost Coast-to-Coast character.

"What about coffee?" Nina grinned.

"Hey kids," he said in his cultured voice, "too much coffee makes me jittery."

She laughed out loud. "So, are you *very* mad at me?" She supposed it was mean of her to tell everybody that he was a devoted fan of the silly and sweet but dumb little alien and his family and friends.

"Well, my Nina," he spoke slowly, lifting her hand to his mouth and kissing it lingeringly, his other hand on the wheel, "I think I am so angry that I will make you watch the Brak show with me Tuesday night wearing nothing but my new 'Don't Dance in the Tub' tee shirt. It sports a picture of a large green mantis glaring. He has a bruise on his hind shell."

Nina was giggling so hard that tears ran down her face. She almost missed the fact that they had stopped. Vasile walked around and opened her car door, moving in front of a valet to do it. He helped her to her feet and into his arms

"Worry not, sweet Nina," he murmured, dropping a teasing kiss on her mouth. "I have plenty of marshmallow chickens for you to eat during the show."

When they entered the concert hall where the singer was performing, she and Vasile were escorted to seats up front near the stage. Nightclub seating had been organized there and Nina was seated at a table with Vasile and offered drinks.

She couldn't believe the service and attention he received. He'd explained that Velicescu Finance supported the series of concerts and the concert venue itself.

Almost as soon as the singer began performing, Nina was lost in the music and fighting herself to stay in her seat. She'd always been weak to good music and wanted to move with it.

Surprising her completely, Vasile pulled her from her seat and back into his body. He began swaying to the music, his arms encircling her waist while she moved with him. With her derriere resting in the cradle of his hips, she couldn't miss his swollen erection.

"Vasile," she whispered.

"Worry not, *meu inimã*, you are safe with me," he murmured into her ear.

"Vasile, I don't want to tease you or make you uncomfortable." she worried.

"Nina, I will not hide the fact that I find you attractive and I want very much to make love to you." He kissed her throat and hugged her tighter for a second, rolling his hips against her bottom. "Simply because I feel something does not mean I have to act upon it." He chuckled. "You have not yet turned me into a savage beast."

Still, Nina worried. "I feel bad about teasing you, Vasile," she told him.

"You tease me by covering that delectable body with clothing every day, my Nina. Hush, dance with me." He turned her to him and they pressed against each other, moving with the throbbing saxophone.

When the concert ended, Vasile led her backstage and introduced her to the performer and his band. To Nina's surprise, the singer and his girlfriend joined them for a light supper. Several people stopped by their table and Vasile kept a proprietary arm around Nina most of the evening.

Nina was fighting a severe case of nerves when Vasile drove her home later. *What was expected of her? Should she kiss him? Invite him in?*

"Calm yourself, little Nina," Vasile purred, walking her to her door. "I would be pleased to have from you a kiss for goodnight before I leave?" His voice flowed over her like warm scented oil.

Nina stood on her tiptoes and braced her hands on his solid chest. "I had a wonderful time, Vasile, and I enjoyed your company very much."

His face, angled down toward her and she kissed his bottom lip. It was smooth and soft. She wanted to do it again. He lowered his head an inch more and she pressed her lips against his, touching them, his lower lip first and then his upper lip, with her tongue.

Vasile parted his lips against hers and wrapped his arms around her. Nina shyly eased her tongue into his mouth exploring his teeth. She slipped past them and stroked his tongue with hers.

Vasile groaned and took over the kiss. Nina was overwhelmed, losing herself in his taste, his feel, and his demanding mouth. By the time Vasile pulled his face away from hers, she would have fallen if she hadn't been clinging to him still.

"I, too, had a wonderful date, my Nina. Please to come out with me again?"

His voice sounded like sandpaper and black velvet to her sensitive ears.

"I'd like that very much, Vasile," she responded huskily.

He helped her in the door and made sure she locked it. Nina fought the ache in her heart as she watched him stride away into the night.

* * * *

Nina and Vasile worked closely together but she found herself thinking of them more and more as a couple. It had been two weeks since their date and he'd asked her out on numerous occasions.

One Monday night, near the end of a quiet dinner, Vasile asked her if she had plans for that weekend.

"There is a large dinner party coming up that I attend each year. It could be considered a business event, I suppose." He leaned back and crossed one ankle over the other.

"I did avoid it last year, now that I think back. I realize that the last time I attended, you were there." His gaze was still focused on her.

"Vasile, do you mean the event my old firm hosts each year?" she asked, surprised.

Nodding, he said, "I remember that you were there for a few reasons, not the least of which is how beautiful you looked that night."

Nina was shocked. He'd thought her attractive enough to remember her all this time? He thought she'd looked beautiful that night? She knew she'd changed since then. Unaccountably, she wondered if that meant he didn't find her beautiful anymore.

His amused male chuckle and twinkling jet eyes confused her for a moment. It was as if he'd heard her thoughts. She shrugged the idea off.

"I remember bumping you as we entered the gala

54

and thinking I had hurt you. When I came to see if I had, you were contending with a couple of lowlife insects. You were handling them expertly, I might add" he grinned.

She smiled back at him. "I'm afraid I don't remember that very clearly. That must have been Tweedle-dee and Tweedle-dum." She smiled at him and added, "That's not their real names…"

He seemed to experience a coughing fit and she started to hail a waiter to get him some water.

"No, Nina, please, it has passed. I bring this dinner up for a reason." She was a little concerned again. "It would mean much to me if you will join me. We will go there Friday instead of work. You can visit old friends and family, perhaps?"

Nina remembered the last time she'd attended the party he now mentioned.

That evening, upon arriving at the party, Nina had waited in the hotel foyer for her best friend Jason. After several minutes, she'd felt a strange prickling sensation on the back of her neck and turned.

Jason had been standing against a column staring at her. When their eyes met, he'd grinned and straightened, walking toward her.

"God, you're beautiful," Jason had murmured, walking up. Pulling her into his arms, he'd kissed her cheek.

"You look like six feet of hot sex in a suit, yourself, big boy," she'd flirted, caressing his cheek and ear with a manicured finger and lightly flicking the tiny hoop he wore.

"Shall we?" he'd asked, taking her hand.

They'd entered the main room bumping some people going through the doors at the same time. She remembered waiting when Jason had gone to get them a drink.

Standing alone, she'd attracted the attention of the men Vasile had just referred to as lowlife insects. They usually made lewd comments to her, evidently believing she'd go out with one of them if they demeaned her.

"Hey, Ice Lady," said the guy she thought of as Tweedle-dee "You look good tonight! Want to come home with me and fuck my brains out?"

She'd looked at him a minute and responded, "I don't need to. Apparently someone has already beaten me to it." He'd stared at her, confused. She turned away.

His friend, Tweedle-dum had reached for her and she'd asked, "What am I, flypaper for losers?"

Right then, Jason had returned with drinks for them. Nina remembered the whiskey and how much better she'd felt after drinking it. She couldn't forget what had happened when she had left the party with Jason.   "I wanted to talk to you tonight, Nina, so I parked quite a ways away," he had explained, gripping her hand tightly as they walked down the dark streets.

Stopping, Nina had jerked hard on both his hands. "Jason," she'd asked sternly, "what's on your mind?"

On a deep breath Jason had asked, "He came last night, didn't he?"

She didn't pretend not to understand that he was referring to her Midnight Guardian. "Yes, he came," she'd said honestly.

"When he first started coming to you, I was glad," Jason had told her. "I wanted you to have a regular life. I wanted you to have what I had. I had a lot of sex, Nina, and I felt guilty."

She'd said nothing.

"When I first learned that he was there for you, I was grateful. I knew I couldn't help you with what had happened to you. I just wanted to have fun and have sex. I also wanted you to be my friend," he went on. "Thanks to your mysterious lover, I had all that I wanted and you did, too."

"So?" questioned Nina, "what's wrong now?"

"Sweet, beautiful Nina. Life cannot be lived in a vacuum. I know it and you're elusive lover knows it. You are the only one who doesn't know it. I think he likes it that way." He'd seemed so sure of himself—knowing just what he meant. Nina hadn't wanted to know.

"Jason?" she'd asked hesitantly.

"Nina, you are my best friend. You are beautiful, you are sexy, you are intelligent, and you are so much fun." He'd kissed her nose. *"I don't really know which way I love you, Nina. I just love you. I can't stand that you are so alone. This man comes to your house whenever he wants and he fucks you."*

Nina gave a cry of argument but Jason growled, *"Nina, it's true and you know it. You're there for me and you're there for him."* Jason had been on a roll by then. *"You are the loneliest person I know. I love you, Nina. I can help you. All he's going to do is fuck you some more. You've repaid your debt to him, let him go."*

Nina remembered that she'd stared into the face of her best friend not knowing what to do next.

"Give me a chance. I'll walk beside you in the light of day. I'll be proud of you. He doesn't even know you, Nina."

She recalled that she'd heard a strange growling sound in her head. She'd known somehow that her lover could hear what Jason was saying and how she felt about it. Obviously, he was angry.

"Maybe it's you I love, Jason," she'd said tearfully. *"Maybe it's him."* The growling had grown louder. She'd spoken louder, too. *"Maybe I love somebody I haven't met yet."*

Jason put his arms around her but she buried her face in her hands. As she rested in the circle of Jason's arms, she acknowledged that her Midnight Guardian could sometimes read her thoughts.

"I don't think I love you that way. Kiss me," she'd

told him.

Jason had lowered his mouth to hers and she'd blocked out the raging, growling sound of her unknown lover.

The kiss had lasted for some time. That's really all she remembered about that kiss. It happened and it lasted a long time. When Jason raised his head from her, she'd stepped back.

"I'm leaving now, Jase," she'd told him, continuing to ignore the growling she heard in her head. "If you find anyone who makes you feel like that kiss just did, promise you'll marry her—or him…" Jason looked at her. Finally, he focused.

"Jason, did you hear me? I'm leaving. Water my plants. I'll be back. Jason?"

Finally Jason said, "Nina?" she'd kissed his forehead, waved down a cab and left.

* * * *

Since that first date, Vasile hadn't missed an opportunity to spend time with Nina. He was almost grateful to Jack Gibson for asking her out in the first place.

There had been times in the last two weeks since their first date that he'd had to warn other men off. Usually a mental image of open graves would do it but sometimes he had to pull out the images of flowing blood and the feeling of death's chill.

He felt that she was growing closer to him and knew that he was growing closer to her. Perhaps now was another opportunity to strengthen their bond.

"Nina?" Vasile called to her. He'd been following her thoughts as she'd remembered that fateful night.

"Vasile!" she started. "I'm so sorry. I guess I let my memories take over. That party was the night I left to visit my grandparents. I had my accident nine days after that."

"Are you okay, Nina?" he asked her, searching her face and her mind.

"I'm...I'm fine, Vasile, really." She still looked far away to him.

Vasile reached out and took her hand. "Nina, you know you can talk to me about it, da?"

She smiled at him. "Thank you. It's just that I can barely talk about it to myself yet."

Vasile let it go. Instead he told her quietly, "It is quite alright if you choose not to attend."

She didn't answer him for a few minutes and he really wasn't sure what her answer would be. Emotions flitted across her face and across her mind just as quickly.

"Um, I think I would like to go. Remind me? When is it?"

"I will pick you up on Friday. We shall stay overnight and perhaps return the next evening following the party. It will depend upon how we feel, hmm?"

"Okay." She smiled. "That sounds lovely."

Vasile was concerned about her. Her thoughts seemed to be in turmoil.

Looking deeply into her eyes, he caught her in his mesmerizing stare. "Tell me, meu dragoste, what troubles you?" It was more than a question. She had no choice but to answer.

Her response shocked him. "I haven't been back there or spoken to anyone from there since my accident."

Chapter Eight

Two days later, Vasile began shouting for Nina an hour after he'd arrived at the office. He hadn't seen her much the previous day and he missed her. He wasn't sure why, but he was feeling uneasy about her. When he touched her mind, she was there, but not there, somehow.

"Beverly!" he bellowed. "Where is Nina?"

"Sir?" she always seemed like she needed to verify that it was him, and that he'd called her.

"When is Nina coming in?" Glancing at the thin watch at his wrist, he saw that it was nearly six in the evening. "Is she in her office? Get her in here!" he bellowed all at once.

"Sir?" she cringed.

"What?" he shouted at the top of his lungs. Seeing her face, he asked in a more normal voice, "What is it, Beverly?"

"I'm really sorry."

"What. Is. It?" he asked only a little more patiently.

"She won't be in for a couple of days. She will still be joining you this weekend, though." Beverly apparently still didn't trust him not to explode but she tried to tell him the truth.

"Beverly?" he asked as if he were speaking to a child. "Did Nina say *why* she wouldn't be in for a few days?"

"Sir? Mr. Velicescu? She said it was a personal anniversary for her. A death of sorts, she said."

Vasile stared at her. *She hadn't said she needed time off. Nobody had died in Nina's family. What could she mean?*

"Sir, she said it was just a personal anniversary of a tragic event that only she would find credible. She told me that she'd learned over the years that it was best to plan for it. She'd never been able to ignore it and…Well, she just won't be in, Sir." Beverly had said all she could.

Vasile turned and walked into his office.

He flipped the calendar open. *Holy hell, there it was.* Eleven years ago, she'd been raped. He didn't have it marked. He didn't know if he'd gone to see her each year afterward. If he had, he was sure he'd expected and received sex from her. *Damnation!*

Every year, she'd told Beverly. For eleven long years, she'd suffered and he'd smugly thought he'd been her benefactor. *A death of sorts, she'd said.*

"Bev?" he said, coming out of his office. Beverly wasn't used to such casual address from him.

"Yes, sir?" she inquired.

"I do not know when I will be back," he told her. "Reschedule everything for tomorrow."

* * * *

When Vasile arrived at Nina's townhouse, he didn't find her easily. He knew she was there. She didn't need to invite him in because she'd already welcomed him in on several occasions.

He felt her and smelled her but it took him a little while to find her. Finally, he tracked her down to the closet in the empty guest bedroom.

"Nina?" he called softly. She didn't have any music playing. She wasn't using any shields against him. If she'd been thinking at all, he would have heard her thoughts.

He found her huddling and shaking in a usually vacant closet. Was this how she was every year?

"Nina?" he whispered, joining her in the closet. She pressed herself into the corner. She was clutching her tiny gray kitten. He could see the fear in her eyes. He was a vampire. He should have seen her fear before now. He just hadn't cared enough to look.

"Nina?" he said again, pressing his body closer to hers. She shook like a leaf in a hurricane.

He gathered her quaking body into his arms. *"Meu*

dragoste, it is I. It is Vasile." He stroked her hair and kissed her. She struggled against him.

"*Kele hai shala,*" *Go away, don't you understand?* She whispered to him hoarsely in Romini, "*Kele.*" *Go away.*

He didn't go.

"*Maybe I can help you,*" he responded to her in the same language. He stroked her back and held her close. The kitten in her arms shook as hard as she did.

"Nina, I will be here and no strangers will come. I am here now. Please, I will go downstairs but please, please, I want to stay." he implored her. He was sure that he had not begged for anything in the last nine hundred years.

"You don't know me," she said to him. "You are a stranger to me. Leave me with my memories, I'll be fine later."

"No, *meu inimã,* you are right, I do not know you." He clutched her tightly. "In my very long life, this has become my single biggest failing. Please let me try to know you now," he implored her.

Vasile kissed her forehead and eased away from her. He turned to leave the closet. Once outside the doorway to the closet, he turned back to her and held out his hand.

"Nina? Will you come downstairs with me? I promise to protect you from strangers." She stared at him with wide eyes but said nothing. Inspiration struck. "Your kitty might become hungry or scared. Perhaps we should take her to the kitchen?"

He saw concern penetrate her desire for isolation. She cuddled the little gray bundle against her chest. Vasile felt a stab of arousal and hunger knife through him. He was actually envious of the cat.

She didn't take his hand but she went down the stairs with him. In the kitchen, she put some food and water out for her kitten. She seemed odd to him – unfocused somehow.

After making them both a cup of tea, Vasile guided her into the living room and sat her down.

"Nina, will you tell me about what has happened? This unhappy anniversary?" he asked.

He knew what he'd seen but he'd never known what her perspective was. Now he hoped she would trust him enough to share her memories and her perspective with him. Every little gift of trust she gave him tightened the bond between them.

Abby the kitten crawled into her lap and began to purr. As she stroked the tiny creature's soft fur, Vasile could easily read the conflict in her mind.

"Vasile," she finally said, "You are my boss. Why..." she began.

"Nina, I hope I have become more than that for you. I want to be more than simply your boss. Maybe we will be very close. I have enjoyed our time together." Taking a chance he said, "Perhaps you, too, have grown to care for me somewhat?"

Waiting for her answer, he realized how much he wanted to know about her. It occurred to him how very important it was to him for her to voluntarily share intimacy with him. He wanted to know what she thought. He realized that her viewpoint mattered to him.

* * * *

Without making a conscious decision, Nina decided to tell him about the rape and about everything that had followed. She had reached a point in her thinking where it didn't matter anymore. She was drawn to this man. She was very attracted to him.

He reminded her quite a bit of her mystery lover. He had the same dark coloring but she'd never seen her lover clearly. She'd never seen him with the lights on. She'd loved a man she never really knew. She did know Vasile Velicescu.

If she could tell *this* man her story, maybe it would help to purge the other man from her system. If it alienated Vasile, so be it.

"When I was sixteen, I was raped," she told him without preamble. "It had been such a good day, too." She remembered aloud. Thinking about it, she found herself recalling little details.

"Tell me, please," he asked with his cultured European accent. "What made such a good day before this event?"

"I had done well on an exam, for one thing. But the best thing was that I'd gotten important information. That's why I was so far from my neighborhood so late that evening. I'd had a meeting." She had a half smile on her face. She was still thinking of the meeting, not what happened after it.

She looked at her one-man audience and smiled.

"I should back up a little. I'm adopted." She saw his start of surprise. "I guess that didn't turn up on my background check?"

He shook his head "no". Taking a sip of her tea, she went on.

"That day, I'd just met a cousin and found where my parents' families lived. I was excited. I didn't notice those guys following me," her voice cracked.

She knew her voice was beginning to shake. Vasile moved to sit near her on the couch. He didn't get too close, giving her support and space at the same time.

"They sort of herded me into an alley and, well, they hit me, they tore my clothes off, they forced me to that dirty ground and..." she hitched a deep breath.

Vasile moved closer. "Nina, may I put my arms around you?" he asked quietly. She nodded.

He pulled her against him and she rested against his hard chest. For the first time in a long time, she felt safe and protected. Stroking her kitten back to sleep, she resumed her story.

"I was mostly naked. I was bruised and bleeding in that filthy alley. They continued to kick me and hit me. The grabbed me roughly between my legs, pinching my breasts, biting me. Finally, they forced themselves on me. I'd been a virgin and had never even had a serious boyfriend. They hit me and punched me while they—you know."

She couldn't say it, she was sure he did know. Tears were running down her face now but her voice was toneless. She tried not to feel anything when she remembered that defining experience in her life.

She rested her cheek against his chest. She felt his hand stroke her hair. It felt so good just to sit like that. She couldn't afford the luxury. She began to pull away.

"Nina, are you afraid of me?" He allowed his arms to fall away. "Do you fear intimacy?"

She knew her face was red now. "I don't fear intimacy, Vasile. There was a man who found me and saved me from those awful guys and he came around afterward. Eventually, we became lovers." She heard him exhale.

"He became your—what is the word—boyfiend?" he asked her.

"I think boyfriend is too inclusive a term. After the rape, he came to see me, sometimes at night. He would sit with me or just hold me. Those times were so special to me. When I went to college a year later, he came." She felt his arms go back around her as she readjusted herself on the wide couch.

"We became lovers then. He was patient and caring and taught me that sex could feel good. We were lovers for almost eight years."

"That sounds like a boyfriend," he told her.

"No, Vasile" she smiled, "A boyfriend takes you to the movies or calls just to talk. You do things with a boyfriend besides make love. You *know* a boyfriend. I guess back then my friend Jason was the closest thing I ever had to a boyfriend," she explained. She felt the growling in her head and slammed the door on it. Vasile jerked next to her.

"I'm sorry, I just..." he gave her a weak smile. She smiled back. "So you no longer see your—lover? You had a fight?"

"No nothing like that. We never spoke." She was embarrassed now and told him so. "I'm embarrassed to say that we never, ever said one word to each other. Not "hi", not "have a nice day", not a single word. You can't fight with someone you don't speak to. I didn't know his name or where he lived, nothing. Never even heard his voice." She lowered her face and covered it with her hand. "In my heart, I was wedded to a man whose name I didn't even know for eight years."

"Hmmm," was all he said. "So if you this was acceptable to you for eight years, why did you end things?" he asked her finally.

"I never realized that I was lonely. My friend Jason knew it before I did. I wasn't in love with Jason or he with me, I don't think. Still, he saw that I was completely isolated. Ultimately, I would have ended up bitter and married to Jason, ruining both of our lives. Or maybe I would have just become bitter and alone, longing for a man I loved but never really knew."

"Perhaps that begins to make sense," Vasile conceded. "So how could you end things with someone you cannot call on the phone or go to visit?"

She smiled sadly. "I don't know if I would have ever ended things with him. I've never made love to another man. I thought I loved my mysterious midnight stranger." A stray tear dripped down her cheek. Vasile caught it with his finger.

"When Jason spoke to me about how I felt—how *he* felt, I went home to think. I went to my mother and father's people. When I was injured and feared dead or brain-dead, my parents—the only parents I've ever known—they sold my little house. They decided that whether I lived or died, the decision should rest with my blood family. I never heard from my silent lover after that."

Chapter Nine

Vasile lowered his lips to her hair. He was learning so much about her. How had he ignored this beautiful, interesting person for so many years? She had been his and he'd only taken from her. Was he as bad as the monsters he'd saved her from?

"Where did you go, Nina?" he asked her. "Did you spend nearly two years in Iowa?" He leaned back and looked at her face, at her dark hair and pale skin and those haunting blue-green eyes. "Ireland?" he asked arching a brow at her.

She actually giggled at him. He was surprised. She definitely had a mischievous glint in her eyes.

"*Mandi's familie is de la România,*" she told him. *My family is from Romania.* "I am Rom. My family name is Alecsandri. Think we're related?" she asked him impishly.

Vasile sat back stunned. That certainly explained a lot. If she was Romani, many called them Gypsy, she'd always had the ability to block him.

The Gypsy people, with their awareness and acceptance of nature's many wonders, were more able to fend off unwanted intrusions. He'd always found her hard to read. He realized that she might have learned some additional safeguards when she'd visited her family. Because of her accident, however, she'd probably been too weak to really use them.

"No, *deget mic drac,* I know we are not related!" He hugged her again.

She *was* a little devil. He grinned down at her. When he'd come upon her in the closet, her first panicked words had been in Romany. Why hadn't that registered with him? Perhaps in his long life, he just answered in whatever language he was addressed.

Although he wasn't Romipen - a Gypsy male, he was Romanian and had lived among the Rom.

The tiny kitten stretched and jumped from her lap. Nina was startled and fell away from Vasile. Snatching her before she could tumble from the couch, he jerked her to him. He had stretched to reach her and suddenly they both lay on the couch with her pinned under him. His body clenched as desire ripped through him. His rigid erection pressed into her thigh.

"Nina…" he whispered, hoarsely.

She lifted her hand and placed her fingers on his lips. He couldn't move.

"Vasile?" She closed her eyes. Opening them again, she asked him, "Vasile, would you make love with me?"

He reached out a shaking hand and smoothed his thumb across her lower lip. *Had she really just said that she wanted to make love with him?* The stalking predator within him demanded that he take her then and there. He closed his eyes and fought his instincts.

"I want that more than I have ever wanted anything," he whispered to her. "Are you sure, Nina?" He'd never asked that before of anyone.

"Yes" she said simply. "But Vasile, I've only ever been with…"

Me, you have only ever been with me…

He cupped her cheek with his hand and lowered his mouth to hers, stopping her words. She parted her lips, moaning almost inaudibly as his tongue slipped past her teeth into her soft, sweet mouth. Her tongue touched and mated with his. He forced himself to let her take the lead.

That was something else that had *never* happened before. When Vasile Velicescu made love, he had *always* taken the lead. *Had sex… He'd never, ever made love to a woman before, not really, not even his beautiful Nina.*

69

She pulled back. "Vasile?" she whispered. He was afraid she'd changed her mind.

Looking down into her bottomless eyes, eyes the color of a tropical sky, he smiled. "Yes, *meu dragoste?*"

"Can I…Will you let me…" she seemed to be having trouble expressing herself.

"*Da*, Nina?" he encouraged her.

"I want to be…on top." Her face couldn't get much redder, he was sure.

Without further ado, Vasile wrapped his arms around her and rolled them over so that she reclined on top of his body. He grinned up at her. Shyly, she smiled back. He felt alive with joy.

"I want to be in charge." She blushed.

Chuckling at her, he spread his arms. "Your wish is my command, *meu inimã.*"

Fighting a smile she ordered, "Just lay there until I tell you to do something."

She slid to the end of the couch and removed his short boots. He was suddenly very glad that he'd dressed casually today. Somehow, it put them in an equal position.

Hauling back on first one boot and then its mate, she removed them and then tugged off his socks. She tickled the soles of his feet and then walked up his legs using her fingers.

"I'm afraid you'll have to suffer while I do all the things I've wanted to try for such a long time. Do you mind?" she asked, stopping at the waist of his jeans.

Mind? Is she serious? He hoped she wasn't about to stop.

"I am honored to pay the price of the fool who neglected you, *meu dragoste,*" he croaked.

She tugged his shirt free of his pants and ran her splayed fingers under the shirt and up his chest. He groaned loudly. For a minute, she flexed her fingers in the matting of hair over his pectoral muscles. Finally, she pushed his shirt up.

"Take it off," she said in her husky, sexy voice. Her words and her sultry tone affected him so deeply that he thought he'd come right there.

"Mmm, mmmm," she groaned, looking at his bare torso. "You look as good as I thought you would." She leaned down and took his nipple in her mouth.

She lathed and sucked his flat nipples until he thought he'd perspire droplets of blood—the strain of trying to control himself was so great. With her lips and hands, she explored his neck, shoulders, and pectoral muscles, all of his chest. She spent a little extra time rubbing her cheeks against the fur of his abdomen while her tongue explored his belly button. Finally, she unfastened his jeans and began to ease them down over his hips. She kissed his flat tummy as she lowered the zipper.

"No panties?" she asked him mischievously.

He couldn't have answered if he tried. It took all of his self-control to keep from grabbing her as her tongue traced the flesh exposed by the opening of his zipper.

When she wrapped her soft hand around his erection, he knew he'd come apart any minute. His cock jumped and swelled in her hand. She smiled at it as if it were magic. She tried it again. Finally, she spoke to him.

"Take these off please and sit up," she instructed politely indicating his jeans.

Following her directions, he pushed his pants off and sat naked on the couch. She slid to the floor and kneeled between his legs. Her fingers moved up and down his calves and thighs, resting just above his knees. Vasile wasn't prepared for the impact of her tongue touching the tip of his penis.

He was still struggling for breath when she wrapped her hand around him and began licking the slit, tasting his pre-come. She squeezed his penis and moved her other hand down to cup his balls.

Looking intently at his face, she bent and licked the top of his cock. Her tongue made long sensuous strokes around and across the head, sucking the tip before gliding to the base.

She played with his balls, cupping and squeezing and all the while, her eager lips held and sucked his penis. Teasing with a long, slow stroke, she lowered her mouth and took his balls into that moist warm cavern. He grabbed the couch cushions and groaned loudly. She moved her hand back to his balls while her searing tongue made its way back up his shaft. Taking as much of him as she could inside, she began sucking him with breathtaking pressure. She moved her hands up and down his length, squeezing him while her mouth moved and sucked on him at the same time.

She began increasing her tempo little by little. Hearing the sucking sounds she made and her quiet little moans, his body reacted naturally, his hips moving with the actions of her mouth and hand.

Her tongue continued to stroke the underside of his penis while she sucked him faster and harder. He felt the growing urgency gather in his balls. He tried to stop her but she was unrelenting, stroking him deeper and faster with her hand and tongue until he came, spurting his semen into her mouth. She drank all of it, licking his pulsing cock, and sucking the last few drops from him. He was overwhelmed and amazed.

When she was finished, she kissed each knee and the tip of his semi-erect shaft. He didn't think he could move. He reached for her to pull her up to his lap, but she scooted away from his hands.

After resting a minute, she stood and pulled her own sweater over her head. She wore nothing underneath it. He sucked in his breath at the sight of her full, perfect breasts.

They were plump and round and tipped with sweet, pink, candy-colored nipples. He wanted badly to feel them and take one into his mouth. His eyes greedily traced the veins leading to those succulent looking nipples.

She reached down and unbuttoned the waist and fly of her jeans, revealing more flesh with each button. At last, she began to push them down and stepped out of them. Under her jeans, she wore a brief pair of gold lace panties. Keeping her gaze on his face, she eased them down.

His breath left him in a rush. He was already hard and pulsing again. In all the years he'd had the use of her body, he'd never taken a really good look at all of her. Over the last two years, she'd matured a little. She was so beautifully shaped.

She crawled onto his lap and took his staff in her hand, rubbing it against her aroused sex. He cupped her breasts, squeezing and touching them. He spread his fingers over her ribcage, feeling the scars from her most recent surgery. He lowered one hand to her pale delicate hip.

Nina moaned and raised herself up so that her moist entrance rested on the tip of his cock. Steadily, she lowered herself onto him. Groaning, she threw her head back and began to rise and sink onto his hard staff, riding him.

She leaned forward and he opened his mouth, catching her sweet, hardened nipple into his mouth. Taking turns, he suckled on one and then suckled the other. Her sheath embraced him tightly and she rose up and down on his cock, reaching higher and aching in her uncertain but eager pace.

He kneaded her breasts, pinching the taut peaks, delighting in her mewling cries. She captured his gaze with luminous aqua eyes. He read desire there and the triumph of womanly power. Groaning, she sat up on her knees, pulling herself off him, and then she thrust downwards, impaling herself on his cock again.

With a hoarse growl, he lifted her almost all the way off him and then lifted his hips and slammed his shaft upward again, filling her entirely, simultaneously covering her lips with his own. Thrusting his tongue into her mouth, he kissed her deeply.

Taking over, his fingers clutched her hips tightly as he guided her body up and down the length of him, creating an urgent, smooth rhythm. His body had missed hers for two long years. He'd squandered what he'd had and he needed her so badly.

She was tight, holding him in her hot wet fiery vice, rising and lowering upon him again and again. And then she was coming, screaming from the intensity of it. She buried her face in his shoulder as her sheath grabbed him and milked him, pulsing around his swollen shaft.

Seizing her hips in a desperate grasp, he surged upwards once, twice, and one final thrust. Closing his eyes, his balls tightened and his body clenched and let go. Vasile groaned loudly as he buried his face in her neck and spurted himself deep within her.

They clung together coming down from their incredible climax. Vasile eased them down to lie on the couch. Still buried deep inside of her, he twined his legs with hers as they stretched out.

"Thank you, Nina," he murmured into her hair. "That was beautiful and incredible."

"I can't believe I just did that," she mumbled.

He stroked her back and ran his hands over her rounded bottom. "I can't believe it either, *meu dragoste*," he said in awe. She was already asleep.

* * * *

When Nina woke late the next afternoon, she was confused and upset. They had made love again during the wee hours of the morning. She had been exhausted and thought for a minute that she was dreaming. She wasn't surprised to find herself in her bed.

Vasile had carried her up the stairs late the night before. She'd awakened in the dark of night, startled and afraid. She remembered him whispering in her ear words of comfort. When she'd relaxed into his arms, he'd kissed her passionately.

Sliding his hand between her legs, he must have felt her body's readiness for him. Vasile had pulled her leg over his and pushed his cock into her wet sheath. She felt her heart clutch when she thought of how perfect it was when his hard length had pumped in and out of her.

Now, her little kitty lay curled on the pillow where his head had rested. Vasile, of course, was nowhere to be seen. She was alone again, counting her minutes.

What would he be thinking about her now? She was so glad she'd taken a few days off. She wanted to shout out that she never indulged in such loose behavior but she guessed she had told him that already. Did he think she was making up for lost time?

She thought about calling him but rejected that idea. There was nothing else to do – she was going to have to quit. She didn't want to give up this job; she loved it, but what other choice was there? She also had strong feelings for her smooth, sexy, enigmatic boss. *What a mess!*

She couldn't work for Vasile Velicescu anymore, not after what she'd just done. She couldn't spend any time in his presence and not think about how shameless she'd been. She'd never get any work done worrying about what he thought of her and hungering for his touch at the same time.

Nina felt the tears prickle at the back of her eyes and throat. She sat up, pulled her knees to her chest and buried her face in them. She was fighting the urge to indulge in an all out crying jag when she felt his arms slide around her.

"What is it? Nina? Tell me what is wrong?" he

asked her urgently. "Nina, talk to me!" he ordered.

She felt like such a fool. She was crying openly now. "He always left. I thought you were gone," she choked.

"Shh, I am here, little Nina," he crooned. "When we make love, I will not leave you alone ever again."

Now that he was here and he held her in his arms, she wasn't sure what felt worse. She was so humiliated at the way she'd thrown herself at him. *She'd practically raped the man.*

"I have to—to—to quit," she sobbed, forcing the words out. Vasile started. "I can't w—w—work for you. I h—h— have to leave here. I c—c—can't see you anymore." She continued to sob uncontrollably.

"*Meu inimã*, you must explain," he ordered firmly.

"I a—a—acted like a s—s—slut!" she cried, sobbing harder now.

Vasile chuckled. She smacked him with her hand, still shaking with sobs.

"Nina, little love, hush. You will make yourself ill." He gathered her against him and lifted her to his lap.

"First, let me tell you that what you gave me earlier is the most incredible experience that I have ever had." He squeezed her. "I will not let you leave me, *meu dragoste*," he told her resolutely.

She relaxed just a little against him. He was so strong and solid. She wanted to trust him and she wanted to count on him. She wanted to love him. On that thought, she started to cry again.

"Nina, listen to me." He held her from him. Taking the corner of the sheet, he dabbed at her tears. "Do you listen to me now, *meu dragoste*?" he demanded. She nodded.

"For many years, I was the lover you described earlier. When the woman whose body I used—when she left me, I did not understand. I never understood what a precious gift I had been given."

Nina stared at him, amazed. This was a big admission for any man to make. Remembering his comments as she'd told him about her past relationship, she realized that he hadn't understood her perspective at first.

"With you now, I have been given another chance. I value you too much to squander this special opportunity." His glittering eyes bored into her own, compelling her to believe him.

Resting her head against his broad chest again, she wanted so much to believe that she could have something lasting with this man. She felt his muscles ripple as his arms tightened around her.

Apparently satisfied that she had gotten over her hysteria, Vasile kissed her and pulled her to the edge of the bed. "I have prepared a meal and coffee." He stood her up. "Come visit with me before I must go to the office, hmmm?"

Nina felt her face going pink again. "I should go to work, too, shouldn't I?" she mumbled.

"You will stay home today and prepare for our party outing tomorrow," he ordered her.

"You are very arrogant, you know that?" She glared at him, trying to hide her amusement.

"It is but one of the many things you love about me, is it not?" he insisted smugly, dodging the pillow she hurled at him as he left the room.

They ate the omelet he'd prepared her and drank the coffee. Soon it was time for him to leave.

"Promise me you will have no regrets? Promise!" he demanded of her.

"I promise," she whispered.

Lowering his lips to kiss her, he teased, tasted, tantalized, and explored her mouth until she thought her legs would no longer hold her.

"I will call you later," he announced and then he was

gone.

* * * *

As the car pulled away, Vasile thought about everything that had transpired overnight. He'd wondered for twenty-four long months why she'd left him. How selfish was he? He couldn't remember what it had been like for him as a human but he was still reminiscent of the man he'd been. How could he not know what he'd done to her?

She'd been through so much and he'd never bothered to find out the extent of it. The rape had devastated her life. Her parents had been clearly left embarrassed and uncomfortable by the tragedy. Her only solace had been a silent taker. And she'd loved him.

He truly had not appreciated what he had until she was gone. He'd find himself worried about her and then he would remember that she was gone. He'd think of seeing her and find he had a gaping hole in his life.

Anyone who doubted the existence of a merciful God should come see him, Vasile thought to himself. He'd been so cavalier about her. When she'd gone he'd been, first, angry and, ultimately, abandoned and bereft. He'd realized eventually that knowing where she was and that she was safe had been anchoring to him. He'd felt rootless when he'd thought her dead.

He thought about the amazing way she'd explored his body and made love with him last night. In the past, he'd controlled their intimacy. Now he understood what his selfishness had cost him. He'd never had such a moving experience with a woman.

For the first time in more than twenty-four months, he'd sipped her life force again, while being buried deep inside of her. Loving her was an incredible experience on its own, but tasting her blood while he buried himself inside of her was without equal. He wished he had tasted her juices but still, he felt like he'd come home with his cock buried deep within her and her life's essence on his tongue.

If he'd harbored any doubts about keeping her with him for all eternity, they'd been erased this morning. When he found her crying and saying that she must leave him he had experienced real fear.

He knew she didn't understand that he really was the man she'd described the day before. He realized he'd have to be more direct with her about his failings. He would do whatever it took. She was his.

Thinking it over, he realized that he had never liked imagining her with another man. Now, however, he understood that he couldn't go another year without her, forget about going another nine hundred years. He would bind her to him. He hoped she wanted it, too. If not, he would end his life with hers. He would *not* live without her.

Chapter Ten

It was an eventful trip from the minute Vasile picked Nina up early the next evening. When he arrived at her home on Friday evening, he found her packed and waiting to go. The driver carried her bag to the car and then returned to Vasile.

"She's having some trouble saying goodbye to her cat, sir," the man told Vasile wryly.

Vasile went into her house. "Nina? What's wrong?" She sat in the foyer with her little kitten on her lap.

"I'm nervous about leaving her for two whole days, Vasile. What if she thinks I don't love her anymore?" She looked at him with distress in her big sea-green eyes.

Vasile reached out and combed the hair from her face with his fingers. He looked at her for a long moment. "We shall bring her with us then, *da*?" he asked.

Her face broke into a delighted grin. She threw her arms around Vasile and kissed his face three times. He found her lips and gave her a light, sweet kiss. Touching her fingers to her lips, she looked at him in surprise, still smiling.

"Thank you, Vasile," she said shyly.

Quickly, she gathered everything her miniscule feline would require and was ready to go within ten minutes. The driver rolled his eyes at the new passenger but was pleasant about the whole thing. Anything else wouldn't have been acceptable anyway.

* * * *

Nina surprised Vasile again during the hour-long ride by asking if he'd join her and her parents for supper at the hotel restaurant. She assured him that she would pay but said that, if he didn't have other plans, his company would be a welcome buffer.

Vasile was pleased to agree but he was a little

confused by her request. Why would she need a buffer with her parents? They'd seemed mild enough in the past. He searched her mind and found that Nina's biological mother had believed that her child would have a better future if she were raised as an American instead of a Romani – a Gypsy woman.

Her natural father had died and her mother couldn't face the prejudices of a single Gypsy mother alone in a strange country. She could have gone back to her parents in Moldavia or even left her child with family in America. Instead, her mother had written a note for Nina and had taken her own life.

When they arrived at the restaurant, Nina's parents were waiting for them. Introductions were made and Mr. Caruthers declared, "Please, call me Chaz! We're waiting for a table."

Nina's mother, a willowy blonde, introduced herself as Vanessa. He was sure the woman's plastic surgeon was on her telephone's speed-dial and was considered a family member. Neither of the elder Caruthers seemed all that warm and loving.

Upon seeing Vasile, the maitre d' instantly rushed to seat their little group at a good table overlooking the water. He ordered two bottles of Tasmanian Pinot Noir, which the maitre d' himself opened at the table. He poured Vasile's glass and opened the second bottle. At Vasile's nod, he poured three glasses from that bottle and placed them in front of Nina, Chaz, and Vanessa.

From what he could tell, her adopted parents were uneasy with her background. They didn't trust Gypsies to begin with and had been surprised to learn of her heritage when she'd been given her mother's letter. The rape when she was sixteen seemed to make them even more uncomfortable with her. Since she'd been injured and nearly died two years ago, her adopted parents had distanced themselves from her more than ever. He knew Nina was hurt by their feelings but it had gone on for some time.

As the small group sipped their wine, Chaz asked Vasile what he did for a living. Vasile had noticed that very little of the conversation was directed at Nina. They placed their dinner order and Nina answered Chaz's question.

"Vasile is the head of Velicescu Finance, Father," she explained. "I'm his administrative assistant."

Chaz and Vanessa gave each other a significant look. "Has Nina mentioned that she's adopted?" Vanessa asked throwing Nina an apologetic look. "Normally, that sort of thing should be private, of course."

"I heartily agree, darling," Chaz said to his wife. He turned and patted Nina's hand. "We're sorry, Nina, but banking? Vasile, Nina comes from…" he paused.

"She comes from Gypsy stock," said Vanessa in a low voice.

Vasile was proud of the stranglehold he had on his temper as he searched for a way to answer them that didn't involve bloodshed. No wonder Nina had asked him to act as a buffer. Scanning her mind now, he found she wished that she'd come alone or not come at all. She was completely humiliated.

He reached over and took her hand in his, moving his thumb back and forth across the inside of her wrist in a calming fashion. He waited patiently for the waiter to place each person's food on the table. When the young man left, he responded to her parents.

"My only interest in Nina's cultural heritage is how it has affected the remarkable woman beside me now. She has always proven herself to be trustworthy as has every person I've ever met of Romany descent."

Vanessa and Chaz exchanged another significant look. "Where did you say your parents were from, Vasile?"

Vanessa asked him.

"Moldavia," he answered tightly. "I am Romanian – Moldavian, specifically."

"You and Nina are seeing one another socially, aren't you?" asked Chaz.

Vasile reminded himself that no amount of mental suggestion would make decent people out of the two shallow specimens seated across from him. When he felt Nina's thumb caressing his wrist in an effort to help him remain calm, he grinned.

He lifted her hand to his mouth and kissed her knuckle. Turning his hand, he brought her soothing thumb to his lips and kissed *it* as well.

"Yes, in fact we *are* seeing one another socially." He lifted Nina's wrist and placed an open-mouthed kiss upon it.

Nina began to smile as well. Soon, she was chuckling with him.

"It is most kind of you, Chaz and Vanessa, to worry one se my financial holdings. Let us enjoy our meal and speak no more of money and ethnic heritage." Vasile smiled at Nina.

"I know what, Vasile, Mother, Father!" Nina gave them all a wide-eyed look as if she'd just had a surprisingly good idea. "Why don't we talk about shopping and golf?"

Vasile wasn't sure what surprised him more: the fact that he didn't choke with laughter or the fact that they did, indeed, talk about shopping and golf until the couples parted company.

As he escorted Nina back to the suite they shared, he was slightly uncertain about what Nina wanted from him. It seemed she was uncertain, as well. He wished her goodnight and gave Abby the kitten a goodnight kiss on her pink little nose. When the door to Nina's room closed behind her, he decided to go and hunt.

Vasile was gone two hours when his restlessness

brought him back to the hotel and the suite they shared. As he scanned Nina's thoughts, he found her awake and restless in the other bedroom.

Quietly, he began preparing for bed, knowing that he would never sleep. It was much too early and he was much too hungry for Nina. Finally, he could stand it no longer.

Naked, he walked into her room and stood beside her bed. She rolled over and looked at him with her enormous deep-sea eyes. She held her arms out to him. Without a word, Vasile lifted her against him, carried her into his room, and lowered her beautiful body to his bed. His mouth covered hers, demanding her response, feasting on her while his hands slid under her loose satin nightshirt.

He moved his mouth down to the pulse beating in her throat. His tongue glided over her delicate collarbone. He nibbled around the curve of her rounded shoulder revealed by the wide neckline of her loose shift. Edging both hands under the shirt, he pushed it up and over her head, controlling the urge to rip it in half and get it out of his way. His slow oral exploration then resumed, continuing over the curve of her breast, pausing to suckle a moment on one pink nipple and then the other.

His mouth moved down over the slope of her belly, across her naked hip, down one thigh and up the other. With his head, he nudged her legs apart and cupped her bottom in his hands. He dipped his face to her feminine core and traced her labia with his tongue. At last, he began to suckle her little nub and dipped his tongue into her center. Back and forth, up and down, his masterful mouth teased her, settling into a small, circular pattern that took her to the edge within moments

He slipped a finger inside her, then two, sliding in and out in perfect rhythm with the even, tantalizing sweep of his tongue. When she began to sing out her frantic cries signaling that she was nearly there, he curved his fingers inside her to press against the spot just behind her pubic bone.

Nina came apart. Vasile pulled his fingers free, replacing them with his mouth. Sinking his long incisors into her, he drank deeply of her blood and her honeyed cream. When her tremors began to cease, he closed the pinpricks and slowly kissed his way back up her belly, her breasts, then to her throat and finally her mouth again.

After kissing her deeply, Vasile gently turned her to her stomach, pulling a pillow under her. He began to lovingly kiss the curving line of her back from nape to tailbone. When he reached her rounded bottom, he spread her thighs and took her from behind, entering her with a slow thrust.

He moved her forward with each stroke, leaning over her, his strokes faster, harder. Speed kept them short and deep. She cried out for more, begged him in unintelligible moans and gasps. Her little animal noises were driving him wild.

He felt her climax rush through her, heard it singing in her veins as her heart pounded in her chest. He sunk his fangs into her neck as she tightened around him, and he thrust inside one final, powerful lunge. His cock began to pulse inside of her, filling her with his hot seed. He collapsed atop her pressing kisses down her spine and against the scars on her back.

Still without a word, he gathered her against him and rolled to his side, feeling her drift off to sleep. Before he closed his eyes, he made sure that he would awaken into human sleep when she began to stir the next afternoon.

* * * *

As Vasile slept the next day, Nina forced herself out of bed. She was having lunch with Jason today. Although she knew she'd see him at the dinner that night, she didn't plan to spend a lot of time with him then. She was Vasile's date and she intended to enjoy it. She'd left a message with

Jason's office right after she'd opened her eyes and he'd called her back pretty quickly.

She pulled on the faded jeans and crocheted sweater that she'd worn the day before and left a note for Vasile. She made sure that Abby was fed and watered with a clean litter box and then she went down to the lobby to wait.

Jason was a little late but overjoyed to see her. Finding her in the lobby of the hotel, he pulled her from her chair and spun her around, clutching her tightly to his body.

Nina heard a low menacing growl and shook her head. She closed her eyes and thought, *whether you are real or a dream, this man will never touch me as you have so please, stop.* The growl was like the shadow of a memory to her and she didn't need a headache trying to figure it out.

"You okay, Nina?" Jason asked in concern. "I'm sorry I didn't get to see you before now. I guess I kind of had my hands full, you know?"

"Don't worry, Jase. I'm fine now and I want to hear all about everything, okay? Don't leave *anything* out," she said sternly.

Together they left the hotel and found a cab. They talked about their jobs and her accident and recovery during the ride. Jason had given the cab driver an address she didn't recognize.

"Where are you taking me, Jason?" Nina finally asked.

"Can't tell ya! It's a surprise!" he crowed.

"You know I hate surprises, Jase," she countered.

He covered her eyes when the cab stopped and kept his hand in place all the way up in the elevator. She didn't want to guess at what other people must think with her pressed against Jason like this and his hand over her eyes.

She heard and felt him opening a door, then he propelled her forward. After a second, he stood still keeping his hand over her eyes. He began filling her in on all that had transpired since she'd left so abruptly two years ago.

"Remember that kiss, Nina?" he asked her. She turned red and shook her head, "no". The hand over her eyes followed the side-to-side movement of her head.

"I'm sorry, Jason, some things are just a little fuzzy. Start reminding me, okay?" she excused herself with chagrin.

He chuckled. "That kiss changed my life and you don't even remember?"

In her mind, Nina could have sworn she felt a sense of smugness from somewhere outside herself.

"Just before you took off, you let me kiss you for the first time ever. It was a mind-blowing kiss, pal," Jason murmured into her ear. "You said, "If you find anyone who makes you feel like that kiss just did, promise you'll marry her – or him.""

"I guess I do remember that, Jason." She blushed. "It was a pretty good kiss." She heard growling again. Mentally she stomped her foot. It stopped. "I remember that it lasted a real long time."

"Well," Jason went on, "I did find someone who made me feel that way. I guess I thought that if I felt like that, she must, too. We had unprotected sex."

He sounded both guilty and proud at the same time. "Meet Felicia, Nina!" Jason removed his hand.

"No *way*!" Nina shouted.

"She's ten months old," he said proudly. "This is Helene. We're getting married in a few months."

Nina burst into tears. She was so happy for her friend. A beautiful blonde woman, Helene, put a squirming toddler into Nina's arms. Nina wrapped her arms around the baby and buried her face in her softness.

"You didn't tell me she was so breathtaking, Jason." Helene's voice held a mild reproof. "You also never told me about that mind-blowing kiss."

"Umm," Jason stalled. "Nina is indescribable." Helene kissed his reddened jaw.

Nina sank to the floor with the baby in her arms and let the child tug at her hair and pull at her clothes. To her surprise, the elegant Helene gracefully floated down next to her and the two women played with the baby together.

Jason took the baby after a while and helped both women to their feet announcing lunch. While they ate, Jason asked Nina about her own life. Since they had already discussed her recovery from the injuries she'd suffered in the accident, talk turned to her new job with Velicescu Finance. Finally, Jason asked about her love life.

"Umm, there's a real guy in the picture these days..." she trailed off thinking of making love with Vasile the night before.

"Spill, Lady!" Jason demanded. "I gave you all the details of mine!"

"Thankfully, no you didn't, Jason," Nina said with a blush. "Well...I have a monster crush on my boss." She casually took a sip of the wine Helene poured her. "I'm going to a dinner tonight with him. It's not work. We've, um, gone out several times...and stuff."

Jason stared at her for a few minutes. "Nina, Vasile Velicescu is...well...he's a dangerous man. He could break your heart."

Nina heard the little beginning growl and ignored it.

"Jason, if he's going to, I guess that's that. I'm not running from this. I'm going to see what happens. My broken heart is the only part of me that didn't get taped back together two years ago. If it breaks again, I think it'll stay broken this time. But, you know, maybe that won't happen."

Jason and Helene promised to find her at the dinner later that evening and Nina caught a cab back to the hotel.

* * * *

Vasile heard Nina getting ready in her room after he awoke. He'd known when she'd returned from her lunch with that blonde womanizer. He would have liked to stop her from going at all but he'd been sleeping deeply when he heard her decide to meet with the other man. While he'd known of her intent, he'd been unable to do anything about it.

Because he'd gone to bed early the night before, he'd managed to listen in on parts of their meeting. It had made him feel very good when she told him, even though she didn't know it was him that this other man wouldn't touch her the way he had.

She had told her old friend that she had a monster crush on her boss. That had made him feel very good inside. Upon reflection, Vasile decided that he had a monster crush on his assistant.

He hadn't been able to follow the entire conversation the two had exchanged but there was something about a child. From what he could tell, Nina had really enjoyed the visit. He decided not to reflect on that too much.

When she came out of her room, Vasile's breath caught in his throat. She had to be the most beautiful woman he'd known in nine hundred and twenty-seven years.

Gowned in a long, figure-hugging, jade colored dress of matte silk, Vasile could barely take his eyes off her. Her shoulders were bare, the plunging halter neckline offered teasing glimpses of cleavage. When she turned, the squared back revealed the graceful line of her spine. He was relieved when she pulled a dainty, lacy wrap over her shoulders. She wore no jewelry. Her shining black hair caught in an elegant twist at the back of her head completed her sophisticated look.

"My Nina, I am proud to be your companion this evening." He lifted her delicate hand to his lips, brushing her knuckles with a gentle kiss. Her skin was warm and soft, and her spicy, feminine scent stirred his hunger for her. "I shall have to remain vigilant so that no other tries to claim you for himself." At that thought, Vasile had to close his eyes to hide the red evidence of his beast flickering there.

"Oh, Vasile, do you know how suave you are?" She threaded her hand through his arm as he escorted her out to the waiting car.

Chapter Eleven

Nina was a bundle of nerves. This entire weekend had seemed surreal to her. First, having supper with her parents, making love with Vasile the night before the way she had, and then lunch with Jason--all of it had seemed unreal to her. Now, walking into this dinner on Vasile's arm after being away the last two years, she was feeling very stressed.

After a brief stop to check her purse and shawl, Nina and Vasile entered the banquet hall filled with sparkling lights and elegantly dressed guests. Drawing a deep breath to compose herself, Nina looked around at the room. Along a far wall, she saw tables filled with a wide array of finger foods staffed by waiters beside them a busy, full-service bar.

Through an archway, another room was filled with tables glittering full of crystal, silver, and fine china. The music playing could hardly be enjoyed over the loud buzz of talking and frequent bursts of laughter

Turning to look at Vasile, she caught his smiling eyes looking down at her.

"I will go and get us a glass of wine. You are not to look at another man while I am gone."

She could tell he was joking, trying to put her at ease. She looked up at him with a smile. His jet-black hair shown in the muted light, and he looked so handsome and sophisticated in his black tuxedo. Tall, broad-shouldered, and vitally masculine, he stood out among the other wealthy, handsome men assembled. He was masculine power and sexuality in the flesh.

"I think I should give you a similar directive, Vasile. I'm more in danger from a jealous woman than an eager man."

Vasile threw back his head and laughed. Designergowned women shot speculative glances at him throughout the room. She watched him surreptitiously as he strode away.

She stood quiet, looking around and taking calming breaths. She didn't know why she felt so tense. She wondered if Jason and Helene had arrived yet.

"It's about time you came back, Ice Lady." she heard a voice say. She groaned aloud.

Tweedle-dee had arrived and slid his hand to the small of her back. She felt her skin crawl. Tweedle-dum rested his hand on her spine just above his friend's hand. Nausea almost overwhelmed her. *Oh, Vasile. Now is a good time to come back...*

"Knew you couldn't stay away. How 'bout a threesome? Maybe you'd like to..." Tweedle-dum's last word ended on a high squeak.

Nina turned and saw Vasile moving toward them. The sight of him made her whole body shudder with anticipation. He moved into the room like a stalking predator. Looking at him, the surge of nameless hunger she felt caught her by surprise. With this man so near, she almost forgot the tormentors on either side of her.

She couldn't see the look in Vasile's eyes but both men dropped their hands from her back and began to edge away. All of the sudden, an awful stench filled the air and the two men all but ran away. *If I didn't know better, I'd almost suspect they'd ... Naw...*

* * * *

Vasile was seething with rage. How dare any man put his hands on *his* woman? He'd heard her thoughts as she'd told him to come back. He had allowed the fools to see the bloodthirsty creature living inside of him, showing them a vision of their own mangled and decomposing corpses. At least one of the vermin had lost control of his bowels.

"What happened, Vasile?" Nina asked

breathlessly.

"I do not like other men touching you, *meu dragoste*, perhaps they noticed? Come, forget the unpleasantness," he purred. "Dance with me now. It has been hours since I have held you in my arms."

"It's been a long time since I've tried to dance formally," she warned him, flushing, as his arms closed around her.

"Worry not, my Nina," he said with his mouth against her shell-like ear. "Just relax, press your body to mine, and move with me."

He burned for her, his body going up in flames as he rested his fingers on her naked back. He could feel her thighs brush against his. She smelled so beautiful and her scent was intoxicating to him.

Just holding her in his arms was as strangely comforting as it was fulfilling. Her slight body felt so fragile against him, he wanted to pull her inside himself and keep her there. It amazed him how moving it was just to hold his woman.

He wished he knew what was bothering Nina. The other man, her friend Jason, had not touched her intimately. Vasile would have known instantly. Still, he wondered, did it have to do with her lunch date? Was she missing her friend?

After dinner, Vasile had introduced Nina to a few of his associates and she introduced him to a few of hers. He'd watched proudly as she conversed with the business people and their spouses on an equal level.

He'd gone out on the terrace for a cheroot with some of his old acquaintances when he lost sight of her. For a time, he'd been able to see her but she'd wandered out of his line of vision. Stubbing out his cigar in a potted plant, he turned and began to search for her.

"How is it that you're more beautiful every time I see you?" Vasile heard Jason say to Nina.

As he approached, he saw the other man take her into his arms. The hated blond man kissed her.

"You look good enough to make a depressed woman give up chocolate, Mr. Man-candy." Nina was clearly flirting with the man. Vasile felt his fangs extend in his mouth.

"If I didn't know you were taken, Sweetie, I'd start to get jealous." That was a woman's voice.

Finally, Vasile got close enough to speak. "Nina, there you are." It took all his control not to rip the throat out of the blonde man who still had a hand on Nina.

"Vasile!" Nina moved over to him with her hand extended. She had a pleased smile on her face. "Please, come and meet my friend, Jason."

With difficulty, Vasile forced himself to extend his hand to the man.

"And this is Helene, Jason's fiancée." Nina introduced the lovely blonde woman he hadn't seen at first.

Looking at Vasile, the blonde woman reached for Nina's hand and squeezed, grinning. Nina nodded and squeezed back, grinning and whispering, "I know, I know."

It was obviously a communication only women were capable of understanding but was a complete mystery to men. Jason confirmed this by turning to Vasile and rolling his eyes.

As the two couples stood chatting, Vasile kept his eyes on Nina. He tried to discern her thoughts but they still seemed jumbled and chaotic. He could tell that she felt genuine affection for both the man and the woman.

He thought he understood some things a little better when the baby pictures came out. Nina told him of her visit that afternoon and enumerated the child's many virtues while the two couples talked.

When at last they left the party, Nina seemed grateful. She still said little as they rode the elevator up to their suite. Before he could pull her against him, she walked out to the balcony.

He joined her, unsure how to proceed. The way she kept looking at him from under her lashes, he wondered if she was unsure as well.

"Did you like Jason and Helene?" she asked him finally.

"They seemed nice," he responded. "I was certain that I would hate Jason."

"Why?" she gasped.

"You described him as the closest thing you have had to a boyfriend." Vasile leaned on the stone railing and lit a cheroot. "You said that you might have married him."

"I also said I didn't love him and would end up bitter if I had. I'm so glad that I like Helene." she glanced at him. "I didn't know you smoked, Vasile."

"Not often," he allowed.

"Their baby is very cute." She seemed to be leading up to something. *Did Nina want a baby?*

"Babies are, as a rule, exceedingly cute." He waited.

"Jason is quite the proud papa, she said with a smile. "Do you hope to have kids someday, Vasile?" she asked. "Perhaps you already do?" *That almost sounded hopeful.*

"No, Nina, I have no children."

She sighed.

Once again, he tried to ferret out what was on her mind but her thoughts were all over the place. He couldn't isolate a single one. Finally, after long minutes of silence, she seemed to have come to some sort of resolution.

"Vasile?"

"Yes, Nina?"

"I need to tell you some things. Please don't say anything until I'm finished. Okay?"

He shrugged. "As you wish."

* * * *

Nina took a deep breath. She wasn't sure how to do

this and she wasn't sure if she even should. Finally, she decided that she needed to be up front with Vasile even if it seemed presumptuous. If what she had to say caused an end to her relationship with him, well... so be it.

"Vasile, I can't have children."

He looked at her, surprised. When he would have spoken, he seemed to think better of it and closed his mouth.

"I don't want you to think that I automatically assume this is a serious relationship for you."

At that Vasile obviously struggled to keep from saying anything. He took a long drag on his cigar and began to choke. Nina decided against patting his back.

"Don't get me wrong, this is a very serious relationship to me." He began to choke again.

"Oh, Vasile, I'm doing this so badly, aren't I?" She took a deep breath. "You're going to be so mad at me. You'll probably hate me and never want to see me again." She turned and looked out over the city lights visible from their balcony.

"I feel so bad. I don't want to put you on the spot." She took another deep breath.

"Okay, here's the deal," she said in a rush. "It doesn't matter if I'm able to bear children because I'm going to die soon anyway. I'm sorry if I led you on in any way."

Resolutely, Nina turned to walk back into the suite. She didn't get very far. One minute she was reaching for the door and the next she was plastered against a very hard body being kissed within an inch of her life. When he finally lifted his head from hers, she felt distinctly lightheaded.

"May I speak now?" Vasile growled.

"Uh huh." she squeaked, nodding. *I wonder which thing I said made him mad...*

"I do not care about children," he gave her a little

shake. "You are the air that I breathe and the blood in my body. There is nothing more important to me than your life and our relationship. Do you understand me?"

Nina nodded mutely. *Maybe he had too much to drink tonight...*

Vasile let out a frustrated roar. Nina was so taken aback that she began to struggle in his arms. He swung her up against his chest and stalked into his bedroom with her. He bent over the bed, laying her down and coming down on top of her at the same time.

He kissed her—everywhere—from the tip of her nose, to the tip of her toes, unfastening and removing her dress, her stockings, panties and shoes as he went. His own clothes seemed to melt away as he removed hers. He made love to her slowly, thoroughly, stroking her abdomen and thighs lovingly, kissing her shoulders, arms, elbows, fingers, licking her wrists, nibbling her hips.

When the need to have him inside of her became too great for her to endure, he surprised her by rolling onto his back and pulling her on top of him. Lifting her above him, he slowly lowered her onto his shaft until he was buried deeply inside of her. Although he kept his hands on her hips, she realized that he was letting her set the rhythm. She raised herself upright, rotating her hips and rising to her knees, easing herself down and up again.

Soon, as Nina tried to move faster to assuage her body's tension, Vasile grabbed her hips harder, holding them still. She braced her hands on his shoulders as he thrust upward and into her, hard, deep, piston-like, until she felt herself come apart.

His savage thrusts continued until the pleasure took him, too, plunging him over the edge of his climax. He poured himself into her, groaning, breathing raggedly as his orgasm played itself out.

She collapsed onto his chest with their bodies still

joined when he spoke again.

"Now, my Nina, I have your complete attention?" He tugged her hair gently until she tilted her head to look into his face.

"Umm, yes, Vasile. Complete attention." *He certainly knows how to captivate an audience...*

"I care only for you. I do not care about children who are not yet born or who will never be. First, we will correct your health problem. I am a wealthy man with unlimited resources. You will not be permitted to die while I yet live." He separated their bodies and pulled her on to his lap, sitting against the headboard. "Do you doubt me, Nina?"

Unable to speak, she looked at him, wide-eyed, and shook her head from side to side.

"After we care for your health concerns, we can once again visit the topic of children." He looked at her intently again until she nodded.

"You will continue to work with me and join me for leisure and social activities until we both feel most comfortable together, yes?"

She nodded again, equally divided between incredulity and amusement. She was struggling to keep her face free of all expression.

His eyes narrowed. "We will talk of this more in the future. Now I will make love with you again."

His hard mouth came down on hers and he rolled her onto her back, covering her body with his. She gasped, parting her lips beneath his, welcoming his invading tongue. After that, Nina could not remember what they were talking about or why she thought they were supposed to talk in the first place.

Chapter Twelve

As he and Nina worked and socialized together, Vasile enjoyed how in tune with him she seemed to be. She didn't need his mind reading skills to know what he was thinking. Time and again she anticipated his thoughts.

More and more he'd learned to listen and pay attention in business when she made recommendations. It had been a scant month ago that she'd proposed a four year plan to expand into the Czech Republic, Estonia, Hungary, Latvia, Lithuania, Malta, Poland, Slovakia, Slovenia and the southern half of Cyprus.

Several members of his staff had argued that this area was only a paltry two percent of the entire output of the EU. They contended that these new European neighbors were not really worth the bother. Vasile decided to give Nina a chance.

Nina had cited sources supporting her belief that those areas would soon be worth quite a bit more in revenues. She argued that, in less than five years, the Central and Eastern European economies were projected to grow quite a bit.

Most of the Eastern Europe banks were well managed and the conservative practices in those areas made the banks a very good investment over time. He allowed Nina to purchase controlling shares in a number of banks there.

He not only had an infinite number of years to realize the recovery of his money, he had what amounted to an unlimited reserve from which to draw. Even so, Vasile was pleased and proud when, in the space of only a month, he was seeing a respectable return on these investments. Every dime would be reinvested back into the area for now, of course.

In celebration, he decided he'd take Nina and the team that had worked on the project with her to a tropical island.

He knew that she loved the ocean and he was determined to spend some playtime with her. They'd take this trip in the next week.

It was liberating to speak to her and enjoy her company. Now that he understood all that he'd denied himself he intended to make up for lost time. Next weekend he would enjoy Nina's company on a beautiful, tropical island.

He was about to walk into his outer office when he heard Beverly tell Nina on the phone that she'd call her office when the boss got back. Vasile was very happy that she wanted to see him. He turned and headed for her office before Beverly had the chance to speak to him.

He heard music through Nina's closed office door and he opened it and stepped inside. As he watched, Nina's body swayed as she danced to the sultry sounds of a Caribbean crooner.

She sashayed in front of him with her eyes closed and he looped an arm around her waist, moving in sync with her. Her eyes flew open, surprised, and he smiled down at her, still dancing. He placed a hand at her back and pressed her against him while he lowered his lips to her forehead.

"You must practice the Samba, as well. I intend that you will spend much time in my arms each night... dancing," he purred.

He hadn't made love with her since the party, but he wanted her, desperately. He touched her mind and knew that she wanted him, too, just as much.

Vasile pressed his cheek to hers and laughed as he dipped her backward. She had seemed taken aback at first by his boldness but now she laughed with him. Neither heard her door open until the sounds of applause filled the room.

Without missing a beat, Nina swayed and glided over to her CD player and turned down the volume.

"I hope everyone has their tropical clothes and excited

spouses ready to go," she said and laughed at the men from the team. The moment was past. Vasile was unaccountably disappointed.

After a brief discussion with the two men who'd arrived and with Nina, he returned to his own office.

* * * *

The executive Lear Jet that she, Vasile and the three other couples boarded fascinated Nina. She was enjoying the new experience until the plane began to leave the runway.

Suddenly, images of her accident returned to her even though she hadn't been injured in a plane crash but a train accident. Instantly, panic took over and Nina clutched at her seat and struggled for breath. Vasile was at her side immediately, breaking away from the group he'd been speaking with. He unbuckled her seat belt and pulled her to his lap, murmuring to her in Romanian.

"*Chavaia! Stop!*" she cried out against his chest. Automatically, she spoke in Romani, the language of her grandparents. "Vasile, *mandi trashd!*" *I am afraid!*

She struggled for control but fear overwhelmed her. Crying and struggling, she struck out at him and tried to escape his restraining hold and the terrifying sensations.

"*You are safe, meu dragoste,*" he told her, speaking in Romanian. "*I am here to protect you,*" he crooned in the same language, rocking her.

The other couples on the plane were in awe of his quick response to her panic. He ordered her a tumbler of whiskey and soothed her in Romanian until she managed to calm down.

"*Forgive me,*" she said to him still speaking in Romani. The others remained riveted as they watched the two interact.

"Please, *meu inimã*, there is nothing to forgive," he reassured her. "You were afraid. We will overcome those fears together."

She'd forgotten the others on the plane for that minute and relaxed against him.

"We will rest a minute and then join our friends," he told her.

When she would have bolted upright in his lap, he restrained her. "It is a long trip, Nina, rest or I will kiss you soundly right here in front of everyone!" He had a wicked gleam in his black magic eyes.

She stared into those mesmerizing eyes and melted. He murmured words she couldn't quite catch and her eyelids became heavy. She couldn't fight the fatigue pulling at her. Against her will, she began to doze.

* * * *

Nina's fear had surged through Vasile like an electric current when the plane took off. He was so joined with her that any swell in emotion would draw him to her. Sharing her unpleasant memories was almost as important to him as saving her from further harm.

He noticed that when her fear was greatest she reverted to the tongue of her biological parents. He wondered if hearing it while she had been in the coma and during her recovery had embedded it into her. He wondered what else was embedded in her mind.

Vasile didn't have to wonder what his administrative staff thought about the exchange between himself and Nina. He listened as the couples chatted.

"Told ya, Bill!" crowed one of the International Banking department heads. "I knew Drac was doin' her!" before Vasile could feel ire over that description, a ringing slap could be heard.

"You're a pig, Michael!" That was the man's wife. " "Doin' her" is what your brother was up to with Mary Jane Blake in the barn that day her father walked in on them. What Mr. Velicescu has going on with Nina Caruthers is beautiful!" she sniffed. Vasile probed… Adrienne, that was her name.

"That was the most romantic thing I've ever seen," squealed Bill's wife, Lori. "She was afraid and he knew it right away. He took her into his arms." She sighed loudly.

"He lifted her right onto his lap. What a chest to cuddle against…"

The third man's girlfriend piped up, "Don't you wish someone would want to comfort you like that? I don't care what language it was…" She fell against her seat, sighing.

"Mandy," growled Ryan, her boyfriend. Then he turned to the other two men.

"It bugs me that you guys would say he was 'doin' her' like that. We've worked for him for a long time and Drac doesn't just 'DO' women. Not like that." Ryan's voice vibrated with anger.

Vasile decided that Ryan Masters, the liaison between International Banking and EU Investments, was due for a raise. He'd known they called him Drac for a long time. The nomenclature amused him. At least they didn't call him Vlad Teppish.

"We've worked with Nina Caruthers for a couple of months now, too. She works her ass off and she's smart as hell. I thought what she said to Soames from Consumer Loans was hysterical. I think Drac was just playing along. It was great! If they got together, they got together after that."

"I know you're right, dude," agreed Michael. "Doesn't matter when they got together… She may be all cuddly with *him* but I damn sure wouldn't want to cross her."

"You got that right, man!" Bill, head of Eastern Europe, EU, Investments, added his two cents. "She's fine looking but she's razor sharp. She *has* guarded his business like a jealous wife. Maybe you should come be *my* assistant, honey. I could use that kind of support…"

Vasile grinned to himself. He liked that his employees

respected Nina for herself. He knew that many of them would not give her credit for her abilities but that could be dealt with. She would always want to work and he wouldn't have her offended.

Conscious that they were being observed, Vasile leaned down and nuzzled Nina's cheek. "Nina?" he murmured.

"*Da, mandi's ves' tacha?*" she mumbled. *Yes, my beloved?*

Vasile's face split in a triumphant grin. The two wives and the girlfriend of his employees saw it. Vasile happily shared the moment with them. He closed his eyes in gladness. His generous mouth still curved in a smile.

"Nina? Come say hello to everyone, *da*?" he caressed her cheek and kissed her forehead.

"I fell asleep? I'm so sorry, Vasile." Sitting up, she straightened her lightweight dress and pushed her hair from her face.

* * * *

What had come over her? She couldn't believe she'd just dozed off like that. Of course, the déjà vu feeling she'd had when the plane began to move had taken a lot out of her. And Vasile had given her that whiskey…

"Hi." Nina addressed the six people seated near the middle of the plane. "I'm sorry I've been so rude," she apologized with a blush.

"You seemed a little rattled when the plane took off, are you okay?" Mandy asked.

Vasile sat next to her and handed her a tall cup of coffee. She smiled her thanks and turned back to Mandy.

"A little over two years ago, I was traveling with my grandmother in her home country and was involved in a train wreck." Unconsciously her hand sought Vasile's. He rubbed his thumb back and forth over the top of her wrist to comfort her. "I guess something about the sensation of the plane taking off reminded me…" her brow wrinkled.

"*A fi la piersică, meu dragoste,*" he murmured. *Be calm, my love.*

"What does that mean?" Adrienne asked.

"What language is that?" Lori chimed in. Their husbands started to speak up and Vasile laughed.

"Be calm is what I said." He chuckled. Looking at all of them, he asked, "What language would you expect Dracula to speak?" It sounded like drak-ool-la in his rich accent. He laughed at the looks on their faces.

Still chuckling, he said, "I speak Romanian and the word Drac means devil in that tongue. Therefore, my employees must think I am something of a devil." he laughed deeply.

"*Tu se beng*, Vasile," Nina laughed at him.

"*Tu e°ti un deget mic drac, meu Nina,*" he laughed back at her. "She called me the devil or the evil. I told her that it is *she* who is a little devil," Vasile explained.

"You are speaking two different languages, aren't you?" Mandy observed. "They're similar but not the same."

"You are very astute, Mandy," Vasile praised her. He noticed that Ryan puffed up proudly. "I am Romanian and Nina is Romani. She speaks *Romanes,*" he clarified. "Our families are both from Moldavia."

"What's the difference?" Adrienne asked but Mandy had seen a hint of distress on Nina's face.

"Don't worry, Nina... May I call you Nina?" Mandy asked. She smiled and nodded. Vasile lifted Nina's hand to his mouth and touched his tongue to it.

"Don't worry about what?" Lori and Adrienne asked together. All three men were nodding vigorously. They wondered what Mandy was talking about.

"Most people call them Gypsies, right?" she asked Nina. "In Romania it's like being Kurdish in Iraq, right?"

"That's a good example. There is no Romany country and the Romanes, who began in India a thousand years ago, have been persecuted and enslaved for many centuries." Nina gave Mandy credit for her knowledge. "There are a lot of myths about Gypsies and I don't want Vasile judged negatively because of me," she stated firmly.

"Hush, *meu dragoste*," Vasile soothed her. "Anyone who doubts your honesty regarding my financial holdings need only visit Soames in Consumer Loans."

There was a stunned silence and then everyone began laughing helplessly.

"How much of that did you hear, Vasile?" a pink-faced Nina asked him when the laughter died down.

His black eyes flashed mischievously when he responded. "I felt no guilt in castigating Mr. Soames the next day since you were true to your word." She sunk low in her seat. *He knew she'd said she wouldn't suck his dick that evening.* He slid an arm behind her back and pulled her up again. "I am certain now that, based upon Mr. Soames' increased profits, you can have any trinket you desire. I would also be happy to contribute to any charity you might name."

She was so humiliated, she turned her face into his rumbling chest and kept it there for several seconds. What must they all think of her? There was no hiding the fact that she and Vasile had a relationship of sorts. *Well, I won't live forever and in a few hundred years who will care, right?*

She pulled her slightly less red face away from Vasile. He handed her the coffee and everyone began to nibble at the snack provided by stewards.

"I decided that a lot of people had already made up their minds about me and didn't care how hard I worked. There's no difference in being hung as a beggar or as a thief." She smiled at the people assembled. "I decided I might as well get some mileage out of it."

The little group chatted until the plane landed. As they emerged from the plane, Vasile stopped Nina on the tarmac.

"Nina, I have reserved you a room for yourself." He looked down at her enigmatically.

She didn't know what she'd expected but that wasn't it. Nina struggled to hide her disappointment and confusion. *Should I be disappointed that he doesn't want to share a room with me or pleased that he hadn't assumed I would want to?*

"Um…okay, Vasile," she got out. He tipped her face up to his.

"Nina, nothing would please me more than to fall asleep with you in my arms and awaken beside you," he murmured. "If you feel more secure in your own room, I will be in no way offended, however, hmm?"

Nina was taken aback. As always, when surprised or stressed, she blurted out the truth. "I only ever feel secure when you're with me…" she said, to her consternation. Face flaming, she stammered, "I mean, um, I just meant…" Hiding her face from his bemused expression, she added, "Oh, hell! I want to be closest to the bathroom and I get the fluffiest pillow!"

His laughter rang out as he lowered his head and kissed her long and passionately. Their audience enjoyed the show thoroughly. They also liked knowing that they were witness to the true relationship between their bosses.

* * * *

By the time each couple was unpacked and organized in their rooms, it was midnight. Since nobody was ready to settle down, they all agreed to meet at the terrace restaurant for a meal. Although Vasile was adept at appearing to eat and drink among humans, he'd sent a case of his own wine ahead. As for eating, it was well known that Nina hardly ate at all so he would "eat" from her plate.

He couldn't be more pleased that she had consented to share his suite. The more he became a part of her life the sooner he could make her his mate.

As he chatted with Michael, Bill, and Ryan about sail fishing and nighttime cruises, he also listened to Nina's conversation with the ladies. When he heard them planning a shopping expedition, he decided it was time to act like a husband.

"Excuse me, gentlemen, I hear the ladies making plans to spend money," he said with a grimace aimed at the men.

"We thought we'd go shopping tomorrow around lunch time while you guys go sail fishing," Mandy piped up.

"Hey boss, I thought you had plenty of money since Soames got off the dime?" Michael teased. "You aren't worried about Nina emptying the company coffers are you?"

"Nina does not need my permission to spend money. She has her own but is welcome to all that I have." He leaned down and kissed her forehead. "I only worry that she takes proper care of her health." Turning to look intently at her, Vasile asked, "Nina, will you be able to go shopping at noon tomorrow?"

"No, I guess not, you're right, Vasile." Nina sighed.

"Perhaps after the heat of the day dissipates, *meu inimã?*" he suggested. "If you go after five, you will be able to spend lots of money and I will arrange an evening dinner cruise for all of us, *da?*"

"That was incredibly diplomatic, Vasile. You did that so well that I have no choice but to agree." Nina wrinkled her nose at him.

The other couples began to head away to their suites between two and three in the morning. Vasile guided Nina down to the beach where they kicked off their shoes and walked barefoot in the sand.

She was delighted with the feeling of the cool sand against her feet and she dared him to chase her in and out of the surf. Soon, he could no longer resist and he scooped her up and carried her to their suite.

Chapter Thirteen

Without stopping, he strode into the bedroom and laid her on the bed, following her down. She was so delicate that, briefly, he worried that he would crush her beneath his larger frame, and that, oblivious of his superior strength, he would hurt her. Nina dispelled that fear, reaching for him, wanting him as badly as he wanted her.

He removed her clothes and then his in a mindless blur. He tasted her; he touched her. No part of her was left neglected by his hunger. When he could take no more, he rose above her.

His body took hers with sweet aggression and domination Nina loved, his mouth frenzied with hunger. Over and over, he surged into her tight sheath. He heard himself moan, overwhelmed with the pleasure and completeness that being in her brought to him. He took her harder, plunging faster, deeper. Around him, her channel clenched, gripping him with satin and heat, clenching and rippling until he had no choice but to empty himself into her.

* * * *

When their lovemaking was over, Nina lay quietly in Vasile's arms. She could deny it no longer. Her body had recognized her Midnight Lover, her Midnight Guardian, all along and now her mind finally had, too.

"Nina?" he kissed her temple. "Did I hurt you?"

She shook her head 'no'. Fighting tears, Nina rolled to her side with her back to Vasile. She was trying to decide how she felt.

Keeping her back to him, Nina mumbled, "I think I need a little air." Pulling on her robe, she made her way out to the balcony. The first hint of dawn was showing itself in the lighter purple above the ocean.

Leaning against the balcony railing overlooking the water, Nina tried to take stock of what she was feeling. She was hurt because he never told her who he was. He'd known that she had felt deeply for the man who'd never spoken to her. Never speaking to her was important, too. *Why hadn't he?* And, when she took the job, he'd recognized her; she was sure he had. She didn't doubt that for a second. She needed explanations and was more than a little afraid of them.

"Nina, what is it?" Vasile hadn't bothered with a robe. He turned her to face him.

Her eyes swimming with tears drank in the sight of him, beautifully sculpted hard muscle, and the perfect amount of body hair. His feet, his penis, and even his earlobes were exactly how she would make them if she were his creator. He was absolutely perfect.

Nina closed her eyes and turned her head. How should she feel now that she could look her fill? Had being able to talk to him and being involved in his life helped her in any way? Had it helped him? She could feel her chin tremble and covered her face with her hands.

"*Meu dragoste*, please tell me why you are upset." He pulled her against his hard body and held her there.

"Why didn't you tell me, Vasile?" she choked out. "I'm twice the fool. I loved you. I was coming back. I was going to speak to you even if you never came back after I did." Tears flowed down her face but she stood still in the circle of his arms.

"Oh Nina, you were never a fool. Only I was the fool." He swept her into his arms and carried her back to their bed, leaving the balcony doors open to the sea.

"Why would you never speak to me? If you didn't want me in your life, why did you hire me? I was an embarrassment to my parents, a burden to my own mother. What was I to you, Vasile?"

"You were my anchor, Nina. I told you before that I had never understood the precious gift I had been given. When you came back into my life, I knew I had been given a second chance." His voice was vibrating with intensity now.

"Vasile, why did you never speak to me?" She couldn't help it—she had to know.

"I thought it was better to keep my daily life and my time with you separate," he answered honestly. "When I thought you were dead...Nina, it hurts me to say the words."

She stared at him. Some part of her wanted to comfort him but she fought the instinct. It hurt her to see him suffer. Her hands shook with the need to soothe away his distress. She couldn't help it and gave in.

"Vasile," she turned toward him laying her hand on his cheek. "Please don't..."

"Nina, you comfort me when I have caused you hurt and unhappiness." He gathered her against him again. "If I had taken better care of you, *meu* Nina, you would not have been injured."

"Oh Vasile, you don't know that!" She wondered distractedly how the tables had gotten turned this way. "Some things are destiny, Vasile." She sat on his lap, stroking his face.

"Do you hear what you tell me, *meu inimã*?" His arms tightened around her and he buried his face in her neck. "Destiny, Nina! You are destined to be with me."

"Vasile, you hurt me. You hurt me badly." She looked at him sternly.

"When you entered my office, I knew you could get to know me and I you. I didn't look the gift cow in the nose. I..."

"Horse in the mouth..." she corrected him absently.

"Horse? I am confused." He *looked* confused, Nina thought.

"It's a saying. Look that's not important, Vasile." Nina

sighed. "I don't know how I feel about this right now. Can't we just go to sleep? My brain is so tired right now." She knew it was the coward's way out, but she just couldn't think anymore.

"May I hold you in my arms as we sleep, little Nina?" he asked her, sounding sad and uncertain.

"If you don't I may not be able to sleep," she whispered, tears prickling at the back of her eyes.

* * * *

Vasile awoke before Nina at around five in the afternoon. When the dawn had come and her tears were still silently falling, he had commanded her to sleep. She wouldn't awaken until he called to her.

He had intended to send her to sleep for most of the day anyway to avoid any chance of her finding him cold and without a heartbeat. As deeply hurt as she was feeling with him, he wondered if she already found him to be without a heart.

"Nina, *meu dragoste,* you should awaken now," he called to her, sitting next to her on the bed.

Slowly, her haunted turquoise eyes opened and she looked at him. She reached and pushed the mass of black hair off her face. Looking at him uncertainly, Nina closed her eyes again.

Vasile pulled her into his arms. "Nina, let us enjoy this day while I show you how sincere I am to make up my previous sins, *da*?"

"Okay, Vasile," she whispered.

He sent her to the shower while coffee was delivered. Before long, Nina joined Adrienne, Mandy, and Lori and the women went off to shop. They all agreed that the men would join them at an outdoor café near the hotel.

Vasile had made the arrangements for the evening cruise and was walking with the others to meet their mates when he felt Nina. A surge of fear rippled through him—

Nina's fear.

He could see her as he approached. A belligerent, rough-looking man had his arm around her neck and a knife pressed to her side. She was choking and struggling to breathe.

I shouldn't have gone off alone, even this short distance! I should have asked one of the others to walk with me—I know I'm the smallest and look like such an easy mark.

He could hear her thoughts as she struggled. Though he disliked that she was berating herself, there was some truth to it. She did appear easy prey, and without him, in the weakened state she suffered, she *was* the most obvious for any attacker. Except that she was never completely alone— he would always be with her.

Without breaking stride, Vasile walked up to the man and grabbed the arm that squeezed Nina's throat.

"Take your filthy hands from my woman," he growled, revealing the red-eyed monster that lived within him. The terrified man plunged the knife into Vasile's stomach.

Vasile crushed the man's wrist in one hand and let go. He plucked the knife from his abdomen and dropped it on to the screaming man. He scooped Nina to him with one arm and closed most of his wound with saliva using his free hand. His actions were so quick that nobody noticed. Of course, he would need to leave a bit of an injury there. A scratch. Too many people had seen him stabbed.

For the next hour, authorities were notified and statements made. When it was learned that Vasile Velisescu's party had been attacked, paramedics were called in and everyone was checked out.

Adrienne, Lori, and Mandy chattered and clung to their husbands, obviously traumatized by the events of the evening. Vasile noticed that Nina didn't say anything. After more than an hour of filing reports and giving statements, the group was finally free to head back to their hotel. More and more, Vasile was concerned about Nina's seeming emotional distance from everyone. When they returned to the hotel, he addressed the shaken couples.

"We shall meet in an hour," he told them, escorting Nina up to their suite.

As soon as he closed the door, Nina was on him, ripping at his shirt. Vasile reached for her, bemused, but she ducked away from his hands. Finally, she exposed the mildly suppurating cut that was all that remained of his wound.

Pressing her mouth to the injury, she began to cry.

"Oh Vasile, I was so frightened for you."

"Hush, little Nina," he soothed, combing his fingers through her hair, "It was a mild cut—a glancing blow at best. I am fine, my love."

She was on her knees with her arms around his hips. Kissing his stomach, she said between sobs, "Please don't ever do that again. I love you so much. I just couldn't bear it if something happened to you."

Vasile lifted her into his arms and carried her to the balcony, settling into a comfortable chair with her on his lap. He kissed her and reassured her, stroking her like a frightened animal until she calmed.

"*Meu inimã*, am I mistaken or did I hear you say that you love me?" Vasile asked her carefully.

"Yes, Vasile," she mumbled into his neck. "I do love you."

Cupping her neck in his palm, he gently tilted her head back with his thumb.

"Please to look at me and say that again?" he asked, his voice strangled.

"I love you, Vasile Velicescu." Tears ran down her cheeks. "I loved you when I didn't know you and I love you even more now."

"I know that I do not deserve you, my Nina, but I will

114

ask you." He reached in his pocket and pulled out the ring he'd had made for her. "Please marry me, Nina, and live your life with me?"

With difficulty, he fought the urge to compel her to accept. In time, he would tell her about himself. Hopefully, she would agree to mate with him for all eternity. In the meantime, he would settle for the pledge of a single lifetime.

"Yes, please, Vasile. I want to marry you." He was kissing her passionately before she could get all the words out.

Slipping the ring on her finger, he told her, "I hope you like it. I designed it for you." It fit perfectly. "The diamond is 4 carats and the cut is called Asscher." He toyed with the ring on her third finger. "I know the band is thick and wide. I wanted it to hold the large diamond and the blue-green sapphires without getting caught on everything." Realizing that he was babbling, Vasile closed his mouth.

"Vasile, it's beautiful. It's incredible," she breathed, staring at it.

"All will know that you are spoken for, *da*?" he murmured, grinning sheepishly. "I hope it is not too heavy."

"The way you have designs cut into the band makes it lighter, Vasile. You can help me lift my hand if it's too heavy." she teased him.

They dressed for their night cruise and prepared for dinner. Seeing that Nina wore a dark turquoise sleeveless sheath, he chose to wear lightweight white linen pants and a long-sleeved, casual, white cotton shirt. It was quite a departure for him but it felt good.

As they approached the other couples, Vasile noticed that Nina was still distressed about the attack.

"I should find that vermin and kill him for upsetting you." Vasile gritted. He didn't care if the others could hear him.

"Vasile, you wouldn't kill someone just for upsetting me, would you?" She knew he'd killed her attackers years ago.

"*Meu dragoste*, I would die for you and I would die without you. To kill for you would be as nothing."

"Oh! My God! That is *so* romantic!" squealed Adrienne. She slapped Michael hard. "And you said he was "doin'" her!"

"No more violence, Adrienne," Vasile admonished her. "Nina has agreed to join her life with mine and become my wife. You will all help us celebrate."

After that, Vasile's amusement was divided between the women and their husbands. The women had descended upon Nina and were 'oohing' and 'ahhing' over her ring. The men were on their cell phones talking to co-workers.

"You won't believe what old Drac did," he heard one of the men say. "He went and proposed to Nina. Better make sure your department behaves itself."

Vasilie frowned as he wondered which department the man was talking to.

"You should see the rock—rocks—on that ring..." someone else crowed. "You'd better hope your woman doesn't see that! You'll be up a creek..."

* * * *

The minute the wheels of the plane touched the ground Nina was forced to make a decision. She had never been to Vasile's home and he wanted to change that.

"Nina, your little kitty already stays at my home. Please to come there now and begin our life together," he'd argued.

Nina had no argument against moving into his home instead of hers. He'd lived there many years and she had only ever occupied three rooms in her house. She wasn't attached to it.

"Everything is just going so fast, Vasile." A nagging

feeling was teasing at her and she needed time to think.

In the end, Nina gave in and she went to his home with him. The minute the car drove through the wrought iron gates of his estate, Nina was overwhelmed with the "otherworldliness" of his home and its surroundings.

The word "genteel" didn't quite cover the home and grounds. The lawns were expansive and dogs that looked suspiciously like wolves greeted the car when it stopped. Vasile stepped out and the animals were all over him, wriggling with joy. He helped her out of the car and they sniffed her politely and then, seemingly, began to welcome her.

Inside the mansion, marble floors and antique Persian rugs blended tastefully with comfortable furniture. There were paintings by the old masters and other priceless objects d'art over which Nina fretted.

Vasile declared that the contents of the house were simply artifacts collected over the years. After encouraging her to look through her new home, Vasile went off to check his phone messages and email.

Nina wandered aimlessly for a while, taking everything in. In the library, she found some pictures of Vasile's male ancestors. She thought the similarities were remarkable and the nagging feeling in her grew.

Finally exhausted, Nina wandered up to the bedroom she would share with Vasile and went to sleep. She didn't stir when he joined her there.

* * * *

Having returned to work on Tuesday evening after their long weekend trip, Vasile and Nina had spent the next few days catching up. She had more to do since she'd taken time off before the trip. He'd hoped that having her possessions around her had helped. He had noticed her leafing through a weathered diary that morning.

Nina had seemed distracted the last few days but Vasile

had chalked it up to nerves and extra work. Now they were embroiled in what seemed to be a never-ending meeting. He realized that something was on her mind but she was blocking him. He hoped she'd let him know what it was soon.

The meeting dragged on while everyone around them hashed over the contents of spreadsheets, profit and loss margins, worldwide and Internet transactions, and research programs. They'd been sitting in this windowless conference room for at least two hours.

She was uneasy, he could tell. A smile tugged at the corner of his full mouth as he felt her eyes on him again, but he kept his gaze focused on the papers spread out on the table before him. He could hear some of her thoughts. That's how uneasy she was.

"*I think my brain is numb,*" he heard at some point.

As he tried to focus on some of the mental anesthesia his employees were so proud of producing, her little mental observations were killing him.

"*Keep talking. I always yawn when I'm interested,*" she thought while the investment proposal team made their presentation.

She'd steal glances his way. Each time she looked, he heard her shift uneasily next to him. She never caught him glancing back at her.

"*I don't mind that you're talking so long as you don't mind that I'm not listening.*" Inwardly, he groaned. She entertained him, she intrigued him, how he wanted to laugh and play with her right now. He'd give almost anything to ignore this foolish meeting.

He mapped the curve of her swan-like neck with his gaze while he daydreamed of tracing his tongue along its curve and easing his fangs into the pounding pulse there.

"*Converse with any plankton lately?*" he heard after one especially dry presentation. He chuckled to himself.

They'd been sitting here for far too long. He couldn't bear another second. Obviously, that would be too long for her, too. Gripping the edge of the table, he eased his chair back.

"Thank you!" he said out loud while he reached with his mind. "Thank you, Larry. Obviously, a lot of hard work went into your presentation. Nina? Anything to add?"

"Um no, nothing to add just now. I want a disk of that presentation so I can review your research, okay, Larry?" she asked with an angelic smile. Larry actually stumbled as he moved toward her with the disk.

Taking it in both hands, she smiled at Larry again and he leaned against the table smiling and looking down at her, smitten.

"Enough Larry!" Vasile growled, annoyed. "We will break now for a meal if there are no objections? Nina, please come with me." Vasile surged to his feet. Nina stood with him, holding the disk.

He strode from the room with Nina following him nervously. He held his office door open for her and she entered. He locked it and was in front of her before she knew what was happening.

Chapter Fourteen

Wrapping both arms around her, Vasile pressed her backward until her back was up against the door. His tongue took her mouth, pillaging and mating with hers.

He had not intended to do this but his resolve had snapped.

"Nina," he murmured. "You do not know how you make me crazy," he gritted as he kissed her again and again.

His hand trailed up her thigh as she unbuttoned his suit jacket and slipped her hands inside. She tilted her face back for another kiss, which he gladly supplied. He nibbled on her lips until the hand at her thigh found the lacy top of her stocking.

Almost against his will, his fingers splayed and eased up her hip. Finally, they found lace at the top of her hip.

"Nina?" he groaned. "What do you have on under this so conservative suit?"

"It's a princess cut, Jacquard suit but the skirt is shorter than conservative," she argued.

"Nina," he growled in warning.

She pulled her shorter than conservative skirt up so that he could see her stretch lace panties with the seven-inch rise at the hips. He turned her, groaning at the picture created by the sheer lace stockings and the barely there sheer panties.

Looking into his eyes, she flattened the palm of her hand against his erection. She unbuttoned the waist of his suit pants and unzipped his fly, and pulled out his large shaft.

Vasile lifted her and she reached down and pulled the thin crotch of her briefs out of the way. With her other hand, she guided the head of his cock to her entrance.

"I want you inside me, Vasile," she whispered. Resting her hands on his shoulders now, she dropped her forehead to his.

Slowly, he slid his throbbing cock into her. She kept both arms around his neck while he held her hips in his large hands.

In three strides, he walked to his desk and rested her bottom on it. She spread her legs wider as he held her in place. Nina leaned back, supporting herself with her hands flat on the desk. Vasile loomed over her as his hips pumped with a fierce, driving force.

He could feel her orgasm but he couldn't slow down. He continued to drive his cock into her, stroke after forceful stroke. Finally, with one last powerful lunge, he slammed into her and buried his teeth in her pulse. He felt her body climax around him again as she screamed into his shoulder. Quickly after the briefest of sips, he licked the tiny punctures closed.

He gathered her against him, kissing her, and whispering words of love to her. Slowly and carefully, he moved back and pulled out of her, and then straightened her clothing. She stood against him for a long time.

He didn't know what she was thinking but he sensed her mind was once again in turmoil.

* * * *

"Vasile?" Nina finally spoke.

"Yes, *meu* Nina?" he responded.

"I want to ask you...I just want you to be more honest with me than you have been in the past, okay?" She looked intently at him.

"*Da*, Nina, I will answer you and be honest." Was it her imagination or had he just swallowed nervously?

"Do you love me?" she asked him.

"*Da*, Nina, I love you more than life itself."

"From the first day that you came to see me after the rape, I kept track of how many minutes I spent with you. You only ever came to me in the middle of the night so I called it *Counting Midnight*." She smiled wryly at him.

He leaned over to the speaker on his desk and instructed Beverly to reschedule individual presentations from the remaining departments. The rest of the meeting was cancelled.

Nina had seated herself in a chair at the back of his office and he moved to sit opposite her, focused on her words.

"As I was saying, Vasile," Nina went on, "I thought of it as an exchange of sorts. You gave me your minutes when you didn't have to. They were precious to me."

He nodded and continued to stare fixedly at her.

"You took from me the only things I had to give, my body and my blood. I gave them willingly." Nina saw that Vasile was shocked.

"You knew..." his voice came out in a choked whisper.

"I knew but I didn't know. I knew you drank my blood but I refused to think about it. When I was injured, I forgot. It was a lost memory." She looked away for a minute. Looking into his eyes again, she stated, "I need to know what manner of man I am pledged to marry. I need to know what is expected of me, Vasile."

Vasile stared at her for a full minute, unmoving. Finally, he nodded as if he'd reached an understanding with himself. Nina waited.

"You have obviously guessed that I am what is called a vampire. Shall I dispel any myths you have?"

Nina nodded. She knew she was pale. She felt pale.

"I go to church. I believe in God. I wear a cross. As I am Catholic, I make the sign of the Cross with Holy Water. I do not kill people by drinking their blood. I find too much garlic unpleasant because it smells bad, otherwise, it does not bother me." Nina decided that he was clearing up the easy stuff first.

"A wooden stake through the heart would kill anyone,

myself included. The same is true if you remove someone's head from their body. I cannot go out in the harsh light of day but I can be awake during daylight hours, though it drains me. I am ancient so I can go out in the early morning and late afternoon if need be," he continued his explanation.

"What do you mean by 'ancient', Vasile?" her throat was a little dry now.

"What do you think of as ancient, Nina?" he asked her.

"Um, maybe a thousand years, I guess" she told him.

"Good, I am not quite ancient then," he said with a winning smile. She arched a brow at him. "I was born in 1078. I am nine hundred and twenty-seven years old. My birthday is near the end of the year."

"How old were you when..." she tried to ask how old he was when he turned but she couldn't get the words past her dry throat.

"I was thirty-six," he said simply.

"Can you read my mind, Vasile?" she asked.

"Sometimes, *meu dragoste*. Before the accident, I could only read you when you were close by or when you needed me." He reached for her but let his hand drop back to his lap. "I read you now when you are agitated and some other times, but I try not to invade your privacy. I would rather hear the words you would say to me."

She nodded. "Can you make me do things? I mean..."

"I know what you mean, Nina," he sighed. "Yes, I can make people do things."

"I drank your blood, didn't I?" She sat rigidly, knowing the answer.

"You have on three separate occasions," he answered. "You were ill and my blood is strong."

She took a deep breath. It was time to ask the question she had been leading up to. "How come I haven't become like you? Do you want me to?" She waited breathlessly for his answer.

"Nothing would please me more than for you to choose to remain with me until we both decide to end our lives. You have not been changed because I wanted to be sure that it is your choice."

"You were...easing me into it?" she asked acerbically. He shrugged and nodded. "How does one change?" she asked after a minute.

"You become mated to me when we drink one from the other while making love. It is best if we achieve orgasm together as well." He gave her a small smile.

"Really?" she breathed. She hadn't heard that part before.

"There are other ways but they can be...messy."

Nina considered this for a minute. She stood. He stood facing her.

"I need to go and think about this, Vasile," she told him.

"*Nina.*" His voice sounded strained.

"I'm not going to Moldavia, Vasile, only for a walk downtown. I need to think about this." She wrapped her arms around her middle and turned toward the door.

"Nina?" he called softly. She turned to look at him. "I am with you, always."

She nodded.

* * * *

Vasile paced the halls of his office building trying to keep an 'eye' on Nina and still pay attention to where he was going. As he walked, he heard some of his employees talking.

"Whaddaya think's going on? They've been in there a long time," he heard.

"Think they're fuckin'?" That Soames would never learn. Vasile was in the mood to teach him.

"Soames," he growled. The man nearly fell out of his chair. "Whom did you suspect of fucking?" His voice was low and menacing.

"Sir, I didn't know you were there!" Vasile arched a brow at him. "I mean, I, I..."

"Mr. Soames, if you would complete your work and pay attention to your own department, you would not have time to ask inane questions. Perhaps you are unhappy in your job..."

"No, Sir! I'm sorry, Mr. Velicescu, I'm really sorry."

Vasile was bored with his groveling. He snarled at the man, watching him nearly faint, then he turned and stalked away.

Vasile was talking to Ryan and Bill in the hallway near the EU Investments offices when he heard Nina.

"Vasile?" She sounded hesitant.

"My Nina!" He couldn't keep the joy from his thoughts. He hadn't expected her to contact him this way. He had never even suggested that it was possible.

"I guess this does work, huh?"

"It works very well, meu dragoste. I am glad you decided to try it. It is not always possible before the change. But you called to me when you were in the accident..."

"Can I ask you some more questions, Vasile?"

She sounded worried, as if he would deny her. Silly woman. Did she not realize that he could deny her nothing?

He answered her as he ended his conversation and returned to his office.

"Please, I want you to ask. I am eager to answer all questions to your satisfaction."

"Okay. You have to find people and drink their blood, right?"

"Yes, that is how it works."

"How do you know how much to drink without hurting them?"

"It is learned. It takes time."

"Do you drink just anyone's blood?"

"I avoid those using drugs and alcohol when possible.

Also, I have not tasted any woman's blood besides yours since before I met you. I only drink from men."

"I would...would have to learn how much to drink? I would have to drink some man's blood?"

The image of Nina pressing her lips to another man's neck sent him spinning into a black fury. He struggled to regain control.

"Vasile? Did I..."

"No, little Nina, all is well. It is only that I do not like the idea of you drinking from another, especially not another man." He felt her smile.

"So you will provide for me, hmmm? You are a true hunter and gatherer, aren't you?"

Vasile threw back his head and laughed. He was sure she could hear him.

"If I decided not to change, Vasile, would you...What would happen?"

"I would live my life with you, meu inimã, and end my life when yours ended. This happens when couples love each other."

"Oh!"

She said nothing for a time. Vasile began to worry he'd said the wrong thing somehow.

"Nina?"

"I've decided to do it. I want to be like you. I'll be back soon, Vasile. I'm only four or five bl... Oh! A cat...Oh, no! Oh, god!"

"Nina!" he bellowed both out loud and in his head.

"I love you..." he heard her fading voice call.

* * * *

Vasile raced for the fire stairs and out of the building. He found her pretty quickly. She'd been walking back toward the building as she'd said.

There were tire marks on the sidewalk where the slightly dented automobile had left the pavement of the street after swerving. Looking frantically for Nina, he spotted the dazed driver of the car. The woman didn't appear to be severely injured, but people were gathering around the driver's side of the car. Nina was a few feet away, crumpled in the grass, sadly not far from the cat who'd caused the accident.

One look at her and he knew that she was very near death. He wrapped himself around her and sped toward his home. With his supernatural speed, they arrived there in minutes. He ripped her clothing off and did his best to close the wounds that he could with his tongue. He focused his mind on the places she'd been stabbed and tried to repair them mentally. It had been many years since he'd healed anyone in this fashion.

When he'd cared for all the wounds he could find, he slit open the vein on his wrist and pressed it to her mouth. She was too weak to swallow on her own so he massaged her throat, making her take in the blood. When he began to feel weak himself, he closed the wound.

He hoped that he'd given her enough blood. He commanded her to sleep, hoping the blood would begin to heal her along with his healing efforts so far.

Vasile cleaned Nina's battered body and laid her upon the bed where they had yet to make love. He didn't bother to clothe her. Kissing her cool lips, he went out to feed so that he could sustain the two of them.

He found a couple parked in a camper truck pursuing an adulterous affair. Neither used drugs or alcohol so he drank deeply from both. He implanted the idea that their lies and guilt were making both of them sick.

When he'd fed from the man and the woman, the first besides Nina in many years, Vasile hurriedly made his way home again. He'd taken more than he needed so that he could give her life sustaining blood as well.

* * * *

When he returned, Vasile went immediately to Nina. When he searched her mind he found a faint whisper.

Vasile...

It was enough. *Nina, I am coming to you. I must change you. I cannot lose you, Nina.*

He hoped she heard him. She had already told him that she wanted this. He wouldn't be violating her trust, only proceeding a bit sooner and before they'd discussed it as much as he would have liked to. She'd had a million questions, she'd said.

He stripped off his clothes and climbed into the bed beside her. He lowered his mouth to her breast and took it into his mouth. While her face showed no expression, the nipple hardened. He moved to the other one and it tightened immediately.

He felt himself harden. He'd worried that his fear for her would keep him from being able to make love with her now. He plumped and teased at her breasts and lowered his hand to her thigh.

Nina? I am giving my love to you.

He kissed her lips and slid his hand between her legs. He felt her cream dripping over her swollen labia. Moving two fingers into her channel, he found her engorged clit with his thumb. As his thumb massaged her, he felt a flood of feminine juices spill over his fingers. Her body wanted him.

He positioned himself at her entrance until the tip of his cock pressed her dripping lips. He began to push himself inside of her, feeling her stretch and open for him. When he was all the way in, he slid in and out of her a few times, marveling at how good she felt to him even now. He reached up and sliced into the artery above his heart, and pressed her mouth to the wound. Mentally, he compelled her to drink.

Vasile felt himself harden even more when he felt her lips on his flesh. His fangs burst into his mouth. He knew she was drinking. He lowered his mouth to her throat and plunged his teeth into the artery. The taste of her blood on his tongue sent him spinning into ecstasy. Mindlessly, he began to plunge. He thrust into her again and again, feeling her tighten around him. As he felt her sheath clench, he felt a light sucking at his chest. He plunged forward in one last powerful thrust and poured his seed into her.

With his tongue, he closed the tiny puncture wounds on her neck. He closed the cut on his chest using his own saliva. He didn't know what would happen next or even if claiming her as his mate would work. She was so close to death. The sun would be up soon.

Vasile had done all that he could so he pulled her cool body into his and allowed himself to sleep. The comfort of sleeping in the room they'd shared since their trip, the same bed, in fact, soothed him. It felt right, with all of her things around him, softening what had been a singularly masculine room to a place where a couple lived. Where he and his beloved slept together; the room where they would continue to sleep together for many years to come.

* * * *

When he awoke twelve hours later, Nina was laying cold and rigid in his arms. Vasile couldn't breathe. *I have lost her. I have lost her a second time.*

Grief slammed into him in an agonizing wave. He grabbed Nina's icy cold body and roared, shaking her like a rag doll. "How could you leave me again, my Nina?" Bloody tears dripped from his eyes. "I allowed myself to love you and now I am alone without you! I cannot live in this world without you, *meu inimã*!" he raged.

Vasile surged to his feet and buried his hands in his hair. With a roar, he strode to the dresser and began grabbing things and throwing them against the wall. First went an antique silver brush, followed by its matching hand held mirror. He snatched up a perfume spritzer and then a decorative porcelain pillbox. One after another, the projectiles burst, shattered, or embedded themselves into the wall.

"You're going to scare the cat, Vasile. And I'm not cleaning that mess up, just so you know."

Vasile froze in the middle of his throw. The Faberge' Egg he was holding dropped harmlessly to the carpet. He turned slowly, stepping on the priceless rarity, and crushing it. He stared blankly at her. She lay still and pale against the bedding. *Had he imagined hearing her voice? Had he finally gone mad?*

"Nina? Speak to me, Nina!" he rushed to the bed and dropped to his knees beside it.

When she didn't respond, he buried his face in the bedding at her hip. For a moment, he thought he was imagining things when he felt something stirring in his hair. Afraid to move, he opened his eyes.

He saw her wrist and arm move over him. Very carefully, he turned his head. Her forearm was in front of his nose and mouth now. He reached out and gently captured her wrist, dragging it to his face. It was warm.

He kissed her wrist and then her palm. He held her open palm to his cheek.

"Vasile? Did you get something in your eye? It's bleeding." She struggled to sit up. "I think you rattled my teeth when you shook me." she sighed.

He rose to the bed and crushed her against him. Realizing that he held her too tightly, he loosened his grip on her. She reached up and traced the tracks of his bloody tears. Her eyes began to fill.

"No, *meu Nina*, do not cry for me. You are here, alive." He was stunned. She had been dead in his arms...unless... *He felt like a fool but how was he to know? He'd never tried*

130

to change anyone before.

"You thought I was dead, Vasile?" she asked, a tear dripping down.

He leaned over and licked it away, erasing it and the track it had made.

"Yes, Nina, I did everything I knew to do and still I awoke with your cold and stiff body in my arms." He kissed her now warm mouth, passionately.

"I was in there, Vasile. I felt you shake me," she snuggled into his arms.

"I am so sorry that I handled you so roughly." He curved his body around her.

Nina leaned up and licked the bloody tear tracks from his cheek. Rising to her knees, she turned and licked his other cheek.

"I felt you make love to me," she whispered. "I couldn't speak. I couldn't even think. I could only feel and react."

"I do not want you to hate me for changing you, Nina, but I could not allow you to die. I could *not*!"

He pulled her to his lap and crushed her against him. She was still and silent in his embrace for many long minutes.

"Vasile?" she said finally.

He pulled his head back and looked down at her. "Yes, Nina?"

"I think...I think I'm hungry." She gave him a small grin of embarrassment.

"Is that so?" he murmured, growing hard against her.

"Um, hmm." she answered. "How do I do this? Will you show me? Will you let me?"

"It will be my very great pleasure, *meu dragoste*." he assured her with a hungry smile.

He gently caught the nape of her neck and pulled her head to his chest.

"You will find the pulse with your tongue and puncture

the artery with your teeth. When you have had enough, you will close the wounds with your tongue. Your saliva contains a healing agent." His voice sounded hoarse.

She nuzzled his chest and her lips found the artery there. Tentatively, she traced it with her tongue, sending fire racing through his blood. She tested her new sharp teeth, scraping his chest experimentally. When, at last, her teeth pierced his flesh, he succumbed to the burning ecstasy of it.

His body was hard and she moved against him, wordlessly entreating him to take her and join with her while she fed. Any tiny shred of control left him as he plunged his teeth and his thick staff into her at the same time. He stretched her channel, pumping into her over and over in long, deep strokes, harder and faster. His body took hers with aggression, claiming her, dominating her.

Around his hard length, her sheath began to tighten, clenching and rippling until he could do nothing else but follow her into ecstasy. Their bodies exploded as one, with a soul shattering depth he would remember always.

Carefully, he closed the pinpricks on her neck as he felt her tongue sweep the heavy muscles of his chest. The two lay wrapped in each other's arms for long minutes, saying nothing.

"I can tell we'll be sharing plenty intimate dinners from now on," she murmured with a contented sigh.

"Yes, *meu dragoste*, I think mealtimes will always be especially cozy and private between us."

He kissed her forehead and cuddled her close. With her in his arms, Vasile knew he could endure another nine hundred and twenty seven years.

The End